SOME PEOPLE

A collection of short pieces

by

JUNE BASTABLE

Published by YouWriteOn.com, 2011

Copyright © June Bastable

First Edition

The author has asserted her moral right under the Copyright, Designs and Patents Act, 1988, to be identified as the author of this work.

All Rights reserved. No part of this publication may be reproduced, copied, stored in a retrieval system, or transmitted, in any form or by any means, without the prior written consent of the copyright holder, nor be otherwise circulated in any form of binding or cover other than that in which it is published and without a similar condition being imposed on the subsequent purchaser.

A CIP catalogue record for this is available from the British Library.

SOME PEOPLE is a collection of short pieces, many of which were composed for the creative writing class at Weston College and also for Woodspring Word Weavers, my local writing group. In the following pages, the reader will become acquainted with an assortment of colourful characters in various scenes of love, lust, innocence, hate, pride and revenge. These provocative pieces represent my personal, often cynical, take on human nature and, in particular, the vagaries and quirks of certain persons: i.e. SOME PEOPLE.

I came to creative writing rather late in life and am indebted to Joy Kenward and Ann Merrin, my tutors at Weston College, for their generosity, encouragement and inspiration.

I must also thank the members of Woodspring Word Weavers (now publishing their first anthology "Tales from the Far Country") for their support and for laughing at my warped sense of humour!

**To the memory of my dearest friend
Michael Minahan
1948 – 2011**

"The Thousandth Man"

CONTENTS

Mrs Frobisher	...	9
Allotment	...	14
Madame Zurita	...	19
Purple and Green	...	29
Sponge	...	34
Baby's Breath	...	40
Ghost Writer	...	45
Buzz!	...	51
To Be Perfectly Honest	...	55
Sleeping Partners	...	59
Angel	...	64
Crumbs	...	66
Twinge	...	71
Drawn	...	75
Anniversary	...	79
Deathday	...	85
One Won't Hurt	...	90
Home from Home	...	94
Pretty Sure	...	99
Other People	...	104
Part of the Furniture	...	109
Rats!	...	114
Snowblind	...	117
Echo	...	121
All Due Respect	...	126
Secretary Bird	...	131
Presently	...	134
Pretty Bird	...	138
Stanley All Over	...	145
Frankly Speaking	...	150
Perfect Pitch	...	155
Regrets	...	161
A Christmas Verse	...	162
Breakfast Time	...	162
Third Age	...	163
Blind Faith	...	164
Not You	...	165
Neutral Ground	...	166
Passing Strangers	...	172
Spoilt for Choice	...	178
Such a Scream	...	184

Some People

MRS FROBISHER

Of course, the annual Quagmire Village Flower Show will be upon us once more, and I am not thrilled to be saddled with the organisation thereof for the fifth year running. No-one else will take responsibility for it, and even the most enthusiastic gardeners in the horticultural society say that I am the only one qualified to do the job properly and that it would be a brave person indeed who tried to fill my shoes. Oh, how they work me, these people! Simply because I'm the doctor's wife and employ domestic staff, they believe I have time to spare, which is simply not the case.

In fact, I run a very tight ship here, with the assistance of Maria Arbutus, my housekeeper, who has been with me for some years. I call her "the chatelaine" which she takes as a compliment – irony is lost on her, I'm afraid – it is simply not in her lexicon.

My days are choc-a-bloc, I have a full diary of engagements and activities, and running a household like this demands much energy and forward planning. For instance, it took weeks of interviews and ensuing investigations before I decided on a suitable charlady, someone who could be trusted around the house to do the heavy cleaning, laundering, ironing, washing paintwork, that sort of thing. In the end I chose Enid Clutterbuck, which was a fortuitous coincidence as she happened to be the only applicant willing to accept the rate of pay offered.

Apart from being an acquiescent individual, Enid is inexpensive to feed; she will make do with bread and dripping at every meal, in fact she prefers it, and consequently is of stocky build, very strong, with arms like a navvy. She appears to have a large family and therefore needs the money and is less likely to take any holiday. I'm hoping she won't turn out to be a pilferer like the previous incumbent who was discovered taking home a quantity of kitchen scraps.

It's not often I express my anger, but on this occasion my temper flared and I flew into a rage. The accused woman protested vehemently, insisting the leftovers were mouldy and fit only for feeding to the seagulls, but she was shaking like a leaf, obviously lying and, anyway, stealing is stealing in anyone's language. We must not allow our standards to drop and, accordingly, Mrs Arbutus was instructed to keep a weather eye out for the correct disposal of uneaten food. She gave me a strange look, but I let it pass.

In order to make Enid Clutterbuck feel at home, I refer to her as "the scrubber"; this sends the poor girl into paroxysms of mirth although she obviously doesn't understand the *double-entendre*. But the creature does seem to laugh a lot anyway, even at things which are sad or tragic – it's quite hilarious to behold, and I do a passable impression of her for the amusement of our dinner guests!

And then of course there's the au pair. I have employed one ever since our daughter Frederika was small as Nanny Montague was never able to manage the child's tantrums on her own. Poor Nanny Montague; she was a real family retainer but sadly we had to put her in sheltered accommodation when Frederika left for boarding school and anyway, to be fair, it was becoming painfully evident that Nanny needed us more than we needed her. I'm afraid facts are facts and I am, as I say, a very busy woman.

However, I do manage to visit the old dear regularly, usually at Christmas, or maybe New Year if the festivities prove too hectic with Frederika home for the holidays.

But I do insist upon retaining an au pair, feeling that such a body can always be useful around the house and, quite frankly, they come so cheap. The current one is a German girl with an unpronounceable name and whom I have therefore dubbed "Brunehilda" on account of her long blonde plaits. She takes it all in good part and doesn't seem to mind helping with bedmaking and ironing. Brunehilda will also take fairly garbled messages over the telephone, and my goodness, her handwriting on the notepad is almost illegible. I intend complaining to the agency as soon as a spare window occurs in my busy schedule.

I have an excellent cook, by the way: Mrs Benedict is known as "Big Bertha" and can be trusted with the menus to a certain extent as she knows what Dr Frobisher likes, but I do take the time to cast my eye over her plans for the week's meals, each Monday morning at 9 a.m. sharp.

As a respite from my onerous domestic duties, I drive into Quagmire Village two or three times a week to meet my friends. Our venue of choice is The Akimbo Arms where they do a wide selection of salads – with oil-free dressing – and their spa water with a slice of lime is simply divine.

Maybe once a fortnight we will motor the ten miles to Quorum Thisbé to replenish our wardrobes, visit a top salon, that sort of thing. It *is* all very time-consuming but, of course, it has to be done.

I am fortunate to be a perfect size 10, and, even though I adore my friends and enjoy their company, I have grown used to being the object of their envy, not that it bothers me unduly because these females are, quite frankly, deeply superficial. However, being a woman of integrity, I overlook their failings.

Some People

Anyhow, during the past few weeks, the topic for discussion over the shredded carrot has been our annual flower show. 'Oh, Veronique,' they say, 'what about Peabody – why can't he do the organising?'

And, yes, I do employ a gardener; a woman in my position cannot risk breaking a nail or acquiring ingrained finger-ends. However, I could *never* trust Peabody with the flower show arrangements. I've dubbed him "Bashful" because of his irritating timidity. His social skills run to a nod and a grunt; I wouldn't like to think the local caterers and marquee chappies were having to deal with him over the telephone: what a ghastly thought!

No, if I want a thing doing properly I shall just have to do it myself. Villagers should be able to depend on the doctor's wife and – me being me – I shall storm ahead, as per. A few telephone calls, a few tatty rosettes and the usual silver-gilt cup – that should do the trick: it's not as if anyone notices; these people are just happy to win anything at all for their pathetic floral offerings.

But I'm never short of adjudicators, oh no! Certain persons adore sitting in judgment over their fellow growers, obviously. In fact, I have to reject one or two of the more arrogant types – we don't want that kind of superior attitude spoiling the friendliness of the occasion.

Actually, I'm now wondering whether Maria Arbutus could be trusted with the task in hand. It occurs to me that she manages to do the flower arranging for the house – seems to be fairly adequate at the task, although I do of course supervise her in order to add the finishing touches with an artistic adjustment of the fern here and there. I shall ask her what she thinks about organising the flower show as a favour to me – but no – a flash of inspiration – I'll simply tell her what to do, and leave it at that. She may even take it as a compliment if I turn on the charm. These domestics can be so gullible. Ha!

Yes, that's what I shall do – delegate the damn thing – no-one will know and I shall be awarded full credit on the day, my picture in the paper, a glowing write-up, etc.

After all, I have more important matters on my mind: for instance, once a week or so, I make a special effort to look my best, ready to greet Dr Frobisher – Freddie – upon his return from evening surgery. As he enters the hallway, he sees me as a living tableau, gracefully tweaking the gypsofila. Then, pretending to be surprised, I quickly turn my head towards him and look askance over one shoulder (my best side, naturally). I am well aware what a pretty picture this presents because I've practised it with two mirrors.

'Veronique, my darling,' he will croon, the anticipatory glint in his adoring gaze indicating his post-prandial intentions. 'Tonight's the night, then! What shall it be; vicar and tart or gangster and moll?'

Well, I'm sorry, but I have to keep Freddie happy – oh yes, he must be kept happy, and fortunately he has love enough for the both of us because, as far as I'm concerned, this is yet another chore to get through, another item to cross off my list of things to do.

Unfortunately, I cannot delegate this one.

ALLOTMENT

I'd always lived in a house with a garden. I loved helping my parents dig the rich moist earth, letting it run through my fingers, planting seeds and watching the flowers and vegetables grow.

Then at the age of twenty-one I fell in love with Alan and we got married. "To Alan and Sandra, the perfect couple" was the toast at our wedding. Being so young, all we could afford was the rental on a top floor flat. It was exciting having our very own love nest, albeit without a garden, and the weekend we moved in, Alan cobbled together some window-boxes "for me to play with" as he put it. This was such a generous, thoughtful gesture, and after that I couldn't do enough for him. I made sure to get home first each evening and, freshly showered and dressed, with just a touch of lipstick and mascara, a frilly apron tied around my waist, I'd be ready to hand him a drink and tempt his appetite with one of his favourite meals.

It was hard work, but I didn't mind as I loved him so and he did help with the washing-up afterwards – a joint effort he said, dabbing the tea towel hither and thither. Yes, life was idyllic, and after dinner we would sit cuddling on the settee with our drinks, watching Sky Sports, before making for the bedroom.

Time passed, and I began to feel exhausted at the very thought of rushing home from work and cooking, so I'd call in at the Chinese takeaway on the corner. Alan didn't seem to notice the difference and wolfed it all down as usual, gradually leaving me to do the washing-up as "there didn't seem to be as much of it these days". Neither did he clock that I was probably still wearing the same clothes as I'd worn that very morning.

At weekends when I had the housework to do, not to mention the seemingly endless ironing, mainly his shirts, he would "get out from under my feet" as he laughingly described it. He usually went to play football with his mates, or that was the story. I never did tell him how much I detest sport of any kind but, even so, he seemed hurt and baffled when I left him to move in with Christopher on his static houseboat.

I took my window-boxes along and Christopher fixed them up on deck. He was eager to start growing things of his own and eventually had several tall plants shooting skywards. I told him I didn't recognise them at all, but he just laughed and said not to worry.

Christopher had long hair and a splendid beard. He collected crystals and joss sticks and put me in long muslin kaftans, strings of love beads and sandals. He said I shouldn't bother about divorcing Alan as we were married in the eyes of God. I took up smoking just to please him, but it made me cough and I began to feel soporific and starving hungry.

Then he convinced me to have a tattoo on my upper arm and also have my ears pierced – he said the nose and tongue would come later as a rite of passage.

However, after a time I grew tired of rice and lentils and yearned to live on dry land again. I realised Christopher only wanted a soul-mate; he had no interest in the physical world and preferred meditating to socialising. He was astonished and cried buckets when I took my window-boxes plus his strange plants and moved in with Oliver who lived in a house-share. Oliver helped me fix up the window-boxes in the communal backyard because the windows in his room appeared to have been painted shut many moons ago.

It was fun when the other tenants admired my green-fingered prowess, and so I was nonplussed when my beautiful plants disappeared only to be replaced by a collection of cigarette ends stubbed out in the soil.

What originally attracted me to Oliver was his boyish quality, the way he called me Mummy instead of Sandra, and his unflagging enthusiasm for life. His innocent pastimes included leaving fake spiders and snakes around the place and removing people's possessions just for fun. This was very amusing – to start with!

After a while, our cluttered room became claustrophobic and my nerves were in shreds because I could never guess what new jape he was planning. For example, he might be springing out of the wardrobe wearing a horror mask or, more subtly, leaving plastic scorpions in my underwear drawer, or, and this was really mean, hiding all my shoes and forcing me to wear flip-flops to the office.

Yes, childlike could be endearing, but childish was definitely irritating.

Oliver dismissed my complaints, maintaining it was only a bit of fun and that I had no sense of humour, but he remained uncomprehending and sobbed like a baby when I left him and moved in with Mark.

Mark announced that women should celebrate their individuality and took me shopping for high-heels, skimpy tops and short skirts and, for bedtime, several diaphanous negligées plus, I must confess, black stockings and suspenders. Honestly, the things I did for him – it was absolutely draining.

And so much money was spent on clothes and dining out that all we could afford was a third-floor flat. Mark wasn't a handyman by any means so I installed the window- boxes myself, much to his disgust. 'Don't ruin your expensive manicure growing all these flowers when I buy you a dozen red roses every day,' he growled, simultaneously preening and smirking at his own reflection in the mirror.

I managed to ignore his skewed logic, but it was the last straw when he wanted me to have double-D breast implants and teeth whitening: I realised all he wanted was some sort of sex object – in other words, a tart.

"C'est la vie" was his only comment when I left him and moved in with Garry.

Garry was "something in the city" but still he insisted we took a poky rented cottage with a tiny sunless paved courtyard at the rear: he said buying property was a mug's game although he never explained why. He loved my window-boxes, explaining that we could grow our own tomatoes and "save a *mint* on greengrocery, ha ha ha".

We hardly ever went out, and I felt aggrieved when he ignored me, seeming to prefer fiddling with his calculator of an evening.

We went Dutch on the smallest thing, and he insisted I pay half the petrol even on a visit to see his mother. He was amazed when I refused to divorce Alan in order to marry him, and was totally flummoxed when I took the window-boxes plus tomatoes and moved in with Brian.

Brian lived in a basement flat but, being in touch with his feminine side, he had turned it into a very pretty and comfortable home. He embraced my window-boxes and joyfully planted herbs of various kinds for use in the kitchen.

Cooking was Brian's forte, but he also took housework and ironing in his stride. In fact he loved nothing more than to dress up in one of my frocks while steam-pressing those fiddly pin tucks on the front of my office blouses.

Brian was a good homemaker, I'll give him that, and how pleasant it was to come home from work and sit down to yet another Cordon Bleu meal. But then I began to dread the nights. I would wait for him to fall asleep before dragging a spare duvet to the settee in order to escape: (i) his snoring; and (ii) the sight of him wearing my lace-trimmed satin nightgown.

Unfortunately, Brian didn't take kindly to having his nocturnal sound effects and fashion sense questioned, and he began to make bitchy remarks in front of his friends; oh yes, he loved putting me down, something he and all the others never remembered to do with the toilet seat!

The day I was moving out and into a bed-sit on my own, Brian flew into a frightful tantrum and came at me with his long painted fingernails. 'Slag,' he screeched, 'adulterer – you promised to divorce Alan and marry me.'

I was in such a hurry to get away that my precious window-boxes were left behind. Oh, sod the window-boxes, I thought, I'll rent an allotment, which is what I did, and my goodness, it's so sweet: it has a neat wooden shed painted green, a vegetable patch and there's also a small flowerbed – life has taken a turn for the better without the stupid self-centred foibles of men to consider.

However! Nearby, on the adjacent plot, there's Jon, a sunburnt earthy chap; he helps me with the heavy work, but what's this – rising sap? Love is growing just like my plants – I will not heed the warning; it's back to nature – who gives a damn if I hate myself in the morning?

MADAME ZURITA

It's surprising the different types of people who approach me for a consultation, even those persons you wouldn't expect to be interested in my kind of business.

Initially, they will come in response to my discreet and anonymous advertisement under a box number in the fortnightly Quagmire News, (i.e. Madame Zurita, clairvoyant and psychologist offers healing and lifestyle guidance). I am confident that people never hear of my services by word of mouth, simply because the whole shebang is completely confidential. Occasionally, a new consultee will turn out to be an existing acquaintance of mine, and it's a source of great hilarity to me when I see their stunned reaction upon discovering that Madame Zurita is actually myself, Abigail Drysdale.

Clients who weren't previously known to me seem nervous of being seen coming to my home, but I reassure them the risk is very small as my house is situated in such a quiet backwater, and there are only three properties on Quagmire Hill on the fringe of the village. My abode faces Mrs Coolidge's house across the road, and further up, perched on top of the hill sits Morass Manor belonging to Dorothea Loomis. A high hedge grows all around my property and so I am entirely hidden from view. My precious poodle Elaine is quite safe there when she plays in the garden.

At first glance, my residence would appear to be a fairly ordinary detached Edwardian villa in the middle-class tradition, but proceeding down the passage, past the sitting room on the left and turning into the dining room, visitors are met by a most unusual sight: the room is festooned with swathes of purple and green muslin, and the walls and ceiling are decorated with silver stars and signs of the Zodiac. On the antique mahogany knee-hole desk sits my precious crystal ball and a deck of tarot cards, which I have the ability to read if a paying customer so requests. The carpet is in shades of purple and green.

One must give the right impression in this business and so I go in for the bohemian look; I wear matching lipstick and nail varnish in a dark plum shade, long purple muslin skirts, glittery shawls and scarves, and green suede ankle boots. My natural Titian hair is long and curly and I set it off with eye-catching dangly emerald earrings. Otherwise, I am low-key.

My clients will occasionally come by car or on bicycles but mostly they arrive on foot as the village itself is within walking distance, about half a mile from here. Otherwise, I do make house calls if people are unwilling or unable to come to my home. However, those consultees of long-standing can also speak to me on the telephone, after 8.00 p.m. but only by arrangement, when my last appointment of the day has finished.

So I am kept pretty busy one way or another, and some evenings I am on the telephone for two hours or more, trying to sort out their problems by "absent healing". In my free time, what little there is left of it, I read extensively on the latest thinking in psychology and also update my scrapbook with cuttings about poodles, dog shows, the occult, the theatre and suchlike.

I am consulted on all manner of things, matters of the heart, career moves, health, property, financial and business. Most of my long-standing clients refuse to make any decision, however important or trivial, without asking for my guidance. Even certain married couples consult me individually, without confiding in each other. It is essential that I maintain the highest levels of integrity in my privileged position of trust because of the intimate things to which I am made privy! It's actually quite amusing. Oh, the trouble I could cause if I were maliciously inclined; oh, the marriages I could tear asunder if I were minded to fan the flames of any conflict, which, I hasten to add, is not within my nature – no, not at all; I am discretion personified.

And these people are only too willing to sign what I call my "Official Secrets Act" which is reciprocal and ensures that every word passing between us is kept as sacrosanct as the confessional. People do love keeping a secret, I find!

This insularity on the part of my married clients does give me a deep insight into their lives which, in turn, allows me to give considered and sensible advice instead of merely groping around in the dark and pretending to see into the future, which, of course, is how I have to work under normal conditions, that is, without prior background knowledge of a situation. It's all a fiddle, really! The more one gets acquainted with people, the easier it becomes to guide them along their particular paths in life because, in general, I find that most members of the public are really stupid and witless, even the educated ones, when it comes to living their lives successfully and/or happily.

One of my ladies is an unmarried actress who lives locally – no names, no pack drill – a real drama queen at all times, to tell the truth. Until my little cottage industry took off I used to tread the boards myself and therefore am still acquainted with quite a few theatrical people, so when this woman sought my guidance on the grounds she had been what we thespians call "resting" for far too long, I advised her to look in The Stage periodical for someone with the initials EG. This she did and immediately spotted a full-page notice inserted by a film producer friend of mine, one Edouard Godolphin – I'd known he was going to advertise because he had asked me to audition! Of course, I was obliged to refuse his somewhat impertinent invitation as I am no longer looking for that type of work, thank you very much!

But, long story short, this actress passed Edouard's audition and was signed up for a series of specialist films being planned in Denmark and, although not too happy initially when reality kicked in, she has never looked back and is busy feathering her nest on the proceeds. She always remembers to bring me an enormous wooden box of cheroots as a thank-you present. 'Abigail,' she says, 'what on earth would I have done without your guidance and advice?' Another satisfied customer, she is never out of work now, and this is a good example of how my business thrives on inside information and a certain amount of amazingly good luck. Serendipity – that should be my middle name: Serendipity, the knack of making happy chance findings.

People say I am a cheery woman and I do try to be on good terms with everyone, whether they be friends, clients, neighbours or merely acquaintances. It's my communication skills, my joie de vivre which comes across, that's how they describe my attitude to life – *it's Abigail's joie-de-vivre*, they say: *if it could be bottled, we would buy some!*

On the rare occasion when I do come across an individual who refuses to respond to my charm (because, really, that is what it is), I pull out all the stops and go out of my way to try and win that person over, which is why I offered to tackle my neighbour's overgrown lawn the other day but I am afraid that she simply turned up her nose, muttering something I didn't quite catch, and went back inside. Later on I was out in the garden playing with my dear little poodle Elaine when I heard the sound of a lawnmower from across the road – so at least my offer did have some effect and got the woman to shift for herself.

The lady in question, Venetia Coolidge, is a sad, drab, grey-haired woman: she lives alone with her cat in the huge house directly opposite mine. In my opinion that Persian moggy of hers (which goes under the name of Perfidia, by the way) isn't a happy cat, so nervous and thin. But really, what a ridiculous name to give a cat – Perfidia! Now my dear little poodle Elaine is just the opposite of Perfidia; such a jolly animal, so healthy and bouncy, and she loves her food. I get the impression that Mrs Coolidge doesn't like dogs, or anything else much, come to that.

But even so, I do worry about the poor woman – it's common knowledge that if she ventures out, it will be only as far as the village shop for her groceries or occasionally to the library, and she must be bored to death rattling around alone in that big house, day in, day out, with no visitors or friends to talk to. I believe the lady has lived in Quagmire for about two years, but no-one seems to know very much about her at all and, as a consequence, she appears to have earned herself the reputation of being something of a loner, a hermit, a recluse.

I was speaking of my concerns to Margery Seligman, the verger at St Quag's, who is of course involved in parishioners' pastoral care to a certain extent. She readily agreed with me that Venetia Coolidge needs to be cheered up, brought out of her shell, made to join the human race, and we both believe I am the one to do it. I mentioned how my offer of mowing the lawn had been rejected, but Margery merely put her hands together as if in prayer, closed her eyes, arranged her mouth in a beatific smile, and pronounced, 'Some fell on stony ground, Abigail – you are a good Samaritan and a caring woman – God will provide.'

Well, I could have wept with gratification, right there and then, although her words did not really make total sense.

So, before deciding on a plan of action, I also spoke to Evie Wildgoose at the surgery just to check her thoughts on the subject. Evie is a great friend and often comes round to see me if we both happen to have a free afternoon. We enjoy a cheroot together, and I invariably take the opportunity of giving her a few pointers, very gently, about personal appearance and hygiene being important in life, especially if she's asked me to sew her back into her nurse's uniform dress after its weekly wash, but it's like water off a duck's back: she always agrees with my sentiments but obviously believes I'm speaking generally and not about anyone specifically! There are none so blind as those who will not see!

Evidently Evie was eager to discuss the Venetia Coolidge problem with me and concurred with Margery Seligman's view that I should take my lonely neighbour in hand because "we pass this way only once". Evie did say, however, that Venetia Coolidge had never consulted Dr Frobisher and furthermore was not registered with him as a patient and so she could not give a professional opinion as to the woman's mental state. We agreed that the said lady could quite easily be registered with another doctor's practice, probably in Quorum Thisbé, ten miles from here as the crow flies, although she does not own a motorcar and the bus service operates only in summer months and then irregularly at the best of times – one really needs a vehicle to travel any distance from Quagmire: this village is quite cut off from civilisation.

Venetia Coolidge must have been on my mind because that night she appeared in my dream. I saw her so clearly, looking strangely serene sitting on the purple velvet chaise longue, my crystal ball in her lap, pussycat Perfidia and my precious little poodle Elaine playing so happily together at her feet.

I woke up with the dream still fresh in my memory and suddenly it came to me, the idea that one might reach Mrs Coolidge's heart via Perfidia because it seems she really is very fond of the animal even if it appears to be somewhat neglected. So I bought several tins of cat food and marched across the road to the house opposite and through the wrought iron gate.

As I walked up the path, a movement caught my eye from the front bedroom window, and, glancing upwards, I saw that a curtain was being hurriedly adjusted. However, I rang the bell more than once and waited for quite a few minutes before Venetia Coolidge appeared and opened the door a crack.

I gave her one of my famous beaming smiles and said with every ounce of charm I could muster, 'Good morning, Mrs Coolidge. I'm sorry to disturb you, but I bought cat food by mistake – here, please take it, think of it as my present to Perfidia. How is she, by the way? I haven't seen her for a while.'

Mrs Coolidge's face was stiff and inscrutable, but eventually she managed to bid me good morning, replying that Perfidia was very well and almost snatching the bag of cat food from my hand. As the front door was closing I called out, 'Perfidia is a splendid moggy – I do envy you.' And that was that!

Drat and double drat! I should have to think up some other means of gaining her confidence and hopefully being invited inside. I couldn't imagine what the interior would look like – probably grey and drab, just like its occupant.

That was this morning, and I still had a full timetable ahead of me, and so I went home to prepare for my first appointment of the day which entailed two personal calls on clients in the village, the first one at the Akimbo Arms, the local public house. I am not giving away any secrets mentioning the venue by name because many people are employed there and it could be any one of them. The Akimbo Arms is run by Percy and Dorinda Grimpenthorpe: they are rather on the vulgar side, as are their part-time staff, if you want the absolute truth, but I never turn away clients on those grounds. I am not a snob.

Afterwards, I had another booking at the Quagmire Inn, where Max and Pandora Bellchamber operate a more up-market hotel-type of establishment, and the same applies there as far as secrecy goes. These people are sometimes too busy during the day and evening to call on me and so I am always willing to make the effort and call on them for an hour. Naturally, I will charge more for personal attendances.

Later on, I decided to stay for lunch at the Quagmire Inn, and Max and Pandora made a beeline for my table, joining me in an exotic vegetarian dish prepared by their talented chef, Francisco.

It was quite amusing really because neither Bellchamber was aware of the other's involvement with my little cottage industry; they tend to work different hours as they don't trust the staff, and are lucky enough to have their respective sitting rooms, or studies as they prefer to call them, where I conduct my consultations.

I have to state at this point with some pride (so kindly keep it under your hat) that the Bellchambers have me to thank for their continuing happy marriage, if they did but know it. By the way, I would never take a meal at that other place, the Akimbo Arms.

After lunch, I had a leisurely walk home in the glorious afternoon sunshine with my dear little poodle Elaine frolicking at my heels.

My next appointment was due at 3 o'clock, and I polished my crystal ball in readiness, positioned some aromatic candles strategically about the dining room, which I refer to as my consultation suite, and plumped up the bean bags on the floor. Some people prefer sitting on a bean bag to lying supine on my chaise-longue. It's up to them to choose – to each his own – I charge the same hourly rate for either.

At around a quarter to three the doorbell rang – oh, dammit, she's far too early, I thought, rather irritably for me – I know the young lady is eager for guidance on her latest romance, but this is ridiculous; why can't people keep to the set time?

I continued applying those important finishing touches to my appearance, tied a sparkly purple and green scarf about my hips, and stepped unhurriedly down the passage to the front door.

I was quite surprised when I saw who was standing on the doorstep. 'Oh, please come in,' I beamed, turning on the wealth of charm which comes naturally to me. 'I wasn't expecting you – I can only spare a minute or two as my next appointment is due very shortly.'

I led the way down the passage, turning left into the consultation suite, and went to stand in the sunshine streaming through the bay window as I am aware that having the light behind me transforms my curly Titian hair into a halo – my aim is for a dramatic effect at all times, or whenever possible.

Satisfied with my position in the sun, I turned round with a gracefully fluid gesture and a questioning expression, ready to ask my visitor how could I help, when my eyes were momentarily dazzled by a ray of light as it flashed and bounced off the crystal ball which seemed somehow to have left its usual place on my desk and was flying through the air before coming down again towards my head in one unbroken movement…

PURPLE AND GREEN

It was only this morning Miss Drysdale rang my front door bell. She flashed her long tombstone teeth between shiny purple lips, handed me some tins of cat food and asked me how Perfidia was as she hadn't been seen around for some time.

I accepted the cans and replied, 'Perfidia is very well, and thank you for the cat food.' Then I shut the door in her face.

Well, I could hardly have ignored the woman, not with my Grammar School education and genteel upbringing. But Abigail Drysdale doesn't give up that easily and as I closed the front door she called out some other drivel about Perfidia which I didn't quite catch.

Really, the impertinence of the interfering busybody – as near as dammit accusing me of neglecting my pedigree Persian!

Hands up; I admit Miss Drysdale annoys me intensely. She lives alone with her poodle in the tall house opposite mine with floor-to-ceiling windows hung with heavy velvet drapes which are kept drawn back, day and night. The road is fairly wide between the two houses at this point, and we also have small front gardens. Along her front boundary grows a high hedge, which she obviously believes blocks out the view.

However, my house is built on a rise and I can see clear over Miss Drysdale's hedge if I stand at the bedroom window balancing tippy-toe on my Lloyd Loom chair and look through my binoculars. She must be a very stupid woman to think she's hidden entirely from my view.

By the way, I would add here that she obviously sleeps in the back as I have never seen a light on in her front bedroom, but I do keep the situation under review.

Miss Drysdale's dog, which apparently goes under the name of Elaine, is often out in the front garden and although the animal cannot be heard from across the road it still annoys me to see the pampered creature leaping about, yapping, trying to catch the birds, and, really, what a ridiculous name for a dog – Elaine!

Lately, Miss Drysdale has been taking up far too much of my time with her antics. People normally keep to themselves in this select part of the village. It's outrageous the way she prances about in a long purple skirt and green suede ankle boots, lacy embroidered shawl about her shoulders and long curly ginger hair, all wild like a forest nymph. That Pre-Raphaelite look is too contrived for my liking. I do know a bit about fine art, by the way.

But one doesn't need a degree the subject to be aware that purple and green don't go. It's a matter of taste, at the end of the day. And she can't be much under sixty in spite of her dangling emerald earrings and plum nail-polish.

Miss Drysdale has many visitors of all types. They turn up at the house from mid-morning through to early evening, but she must usher them into the dining room at the rear as I cannot see any activity in the front of the house, although, naturally, I have craned my neck until it aches.

All this is extra effort on my part, and I almost fell off my perch last week when I accidentally dropped the binoculars. I might have been injured, but came off lightly, sustaining only a small abrasion to the shin. I was pretty shaken up at the time but the daily stress is also affecting my health in general as I am losing out on my sleep because, of course, I have to stay awake until her last visitor leaves. My normal bedtime is 9 pm but I often have to wait up until 10 pm or even later. It's simply not good enough.

I have done my duty as a responsible member of the public and reported Miss Drysdale to the police for being a drug dealer or on the game, what with people and cars coming and going, but the nice station sergeant tells me, quite patiently, that there is no evidence of any wrong-doing. You see? Miss Drysdale is too sly for them. She covers her tracks beautifully.

And it was just a week ago – my God, she accosted me in the street and said, 'Mrs Coolidge, would you like me to mow your lawn for you. I can see it could do with some TLC.'

A purple mist swam before my eyes! 'No, thank you, Miss Drysdale, everything is under control,' I spluttered, stumbling on my way, fuming. She *is* watching everything I do, I thought. The woman is spying on me! How dare she? Her behaviour is out of order. I feel as if I'm being stalked, as I told Sergeant Brocklebank later that day.

It really makes me feel quite angry and irritated when I see her swaying down the street, her hips swathed in a sparkly green scarf emphasising her over-generous girth. She has a kind of contemptuous walk, as if the whole world can go to hell as far as she is concerned. My fingers start tingling with an urge to do her a mischief.

I can, as I say, see Miss Drysdale in her sitting room when she's alone of an evening. She seems to read a great deal – never has the television on, not that I have a view of the whole room from my vantage point. Then again, Miss Drysdale does talk on the telephone, and, Lord, can she talk. I'm pretty sure it's about me. It goes on for hours sometimes. She throws her head back and laughs and laughs, bending forward, guffawing, then head back again, frizzy hair in disarray flying all around her face and shoulders in a ginger cloud. Some evenings, she's on the telephone for such a long time that I don't get to bed until 10.30 p.m. The next morning, I'm like a wet rag, no energy, just tired out. You can imagine how frustrated I am. It's not nice being discussed and sniggered at by other people.

I imagine Miss Drysdale has a throaty chuckle when she gets going, because she does smoke. Yes, that creature is a dedicated addict of the dreaded shredded weed. I was surprised at first because her appearance seems to smack of a "back to nature" sort of lifestyle. But I've seen her in the front garden, cheroot in one hand and a robin redbreast in the other, offering the favoured bird a piece of bread from pursed lips. It's a wonder she doesn't choke the poor feathered beast with her stale breath!

But this afternoon was the last straw. I couldn't believe it when Miss Drysdale's poodle Elaine came chasing into my front garden and made straight for my Persian pussycat basking all unaware on the rockery.

Perfidia nearly had a heart attack, the poor darling, and shot like a rocket straight into the holly bushes, scratching her paws on the prickles. I screeched at the dog, and it ran back over the road and disappeared.

Right, that does it, I thought, and, picking up Perfidia, marched over to Miss Drysdale's house, determined to speak my mind, once and for all. The gate was unlocked. I walked up the path and saw the front door standing ajar. How careless, I thought, the woman shouldn't be allowed to keep a pet.

'Hello, Miss Drysdale,' I called out, and rang the doorbell. There was no reply, so I stepped into the hall and peered into the sitting room. No sign of life! I continued down the hall and turned left into the dining room. Surprisingly, it was festooned with purple and green muslin drapes, fancy candles in holders stood on every available surface and signs of the Zodiac decorated the walls: Miss Drysdale was sprawled on the stained carpet, a livid purple and green bruise on her cheekbone, a crystal ball by her caved-in head.

Perfidia wriggled out of my arms and bounded around the room, leaving red paw-prints in her wake. I did try to help Miss Drysdale, but she was quite obviously dead and my fingers quickly became red and sticky. I picked up the crystal ball, which was encrusted with ginger hair.

I sat down on the purple velvet chaise-longue with green trim in order to assess the situation. Elaine appeared, quickly joined by Perfidia, and they began lapping at pools of blood on the carpet by my feet. I had not the heart to shoo them away.

In a moment or two, I shall telephone that nice Sergeant Brocklebank, but I'm wondering how to explain away my fingerprints which I will have left in various places, not only on this crystal ball which I am still clutching as if my very life depended upon it.

I've covered Miss Drysdale's face with the lacy shawl snatched from the chaise longue just now – but, oh God, I shall never forget the look in her eyes.

SPONGE

As a girl, Doreen Brighouse was apparently devoid of any artistic proclivity; her parents said as much, and everyone else, including Doreen, had to agree. Not a whiff of creativity lurked beneath that mousy lank string scraped back in a severe ponytail and euphemistically referred to as hair.

Nevertheless, Doreen had a philosophical side to her nature and, as she helped her mother with the housework, she would ponder deeply, mostly about the mystery of life and, in particular, her life and the direction it might take if she ventured down an unexplored pathway, metaphorically or literally speaking – it didn't matter which. A favourite reverie would take her along an unknown street, into a strange building containing exotic people, plus a beautiful man who would approach her and say, 'Come with me, I'm in love with you, let me take you away from all this.'

'Daydreaming,' Mrs Brighouse called it. 'Our Doreen has a brain like a sieve, never remembers anything I tell her. No good ever came from daydreaming or from spending Saturday afternoons in the library. It's plain lazy, and unhealthy, being hunched over a book for hours on end. I never read a book in my life, and it didn't do me any harm. She wants to get herself a good job when she's 16, a sitting-down job in an office, of course, not a standing-up one in a factory. Our Doreen is too intelligent to work at a conveyor-belt – I mean, she could read by age four, and, my goodness, she hasn't stopped since in spite of my efforts to get her to do something useful. Then, she ought to find herself a nice steady boyfriend and settle down. She'll make someone a good wife with all I've taught her. There's nothing wrong with that. I was a child bride myself; married straight from the schoolroom, I was. It didn't do me any harm. We've been happy, haven't we, Dad?'

Mr Brighouse, removing his pipe, would agree. 'Yes, Mummy, we have. And kids today don't know they're born. It's worth repeating, so I'll say it again – kids today don't know they're born. They're all spoon-fed and spoilt, the youth of today, even our Doreen. She'll have to pull her socks up and stop this mooning about once she leaves school.'

Therefore, in order to please her parents and, by way of appearing a more comfortable alternative to being swallowed up as factory fodder, Doreen Brighouse readily took a position with the GPO, as it was called in those far-off days, and became a telephonist, or Hello-Girl.

'Our Doreen's got a job as a call-girl,' Grandma Jolly began proudly announcing to anyone who would listen. Naturally this caused a storm in a teacup when Grandma Jolly declaimed the news to Reverend Smollett's guests at his garden party the following Sunday. Doreen didn't understand what all the fuss was about – she didn't know what a call-girl was either, and would not have understood had it been explained to her in words of one syllable.

'Number please,' repeated Doreen for the umpteenth time in her first week at the switchboard. This was pretty boring work with long hours, odd shifts and strict supervisors. After a while, Doreen felt brain-dead and shifted to autopilot mode.

But now it was only one minute to tea-time. She finished the call, tore off the heavy earphone, and rushed to clock off for the precious twelve minutes allowed.

'How do you fancy going on a London weekend break?' they were asking around the canteen table, in between gulping strong sweet tea from thick white mugs and devouring whole packets of custard creams.

'I don't know...' Doreen wasn't keen on upsetting the atmosphere at home, but felt strangely attracted to the idea, never having gone farther than Bridlington, and always accompanied by middle-aged parents.

Mr and Mrs Brighouse looked askance when Doreen asked permission to put her name down for the trip.

'We've never felt the need to go all the way to London, have we, Dad,' was Mrs Brighouse's rhetorical response. 'What's wrong with Bradford, anyway? Plenty of places around here for you to go. We have a nice Town Hall with Hammond organ recitals, and you could always go to the Odeon if you want a posh cinema. You don't always have to go to the local picture-house; and I wish you wouldn't call it the bug-hutch, Doreen – it makes you sound so common and vulgar. With all your reading, you should be able to employ better language than that. I don't know – kids today, they're not satisfied – they want everything. Not like in our day, is it, Dad?'

Mr Brighouse shook his head ruefully; he knew Mrs Brighouse had it all under control – no need to worry about our Doreen spreading her wings, and he went contentedly back to his pipe and newspaper.

'Oh, Daddy, can't you make Mummy see that I want to do more things than she did – the world is changing and we have to change with it. I promise to be very careful and stay with the group.'

Eventually, because they loved Doreen and could not help but indulge her impassioned request, Mr and Mrs Brighouse did agree, with a hopeful, 'we know we can trust you, Doreen.'

But they set down strict rules – always stay together, no stopping up all night, and as long as she shared a room with Janet Bickerdyke, her best friend, she would be allowed to join the trip.

A few weeks later, after a two-day guided tour of London sights, the excited group of provincials had some free time and Janet was keen to go dancing with the others, but Doreen's instinct drew her elsewhere. She knew not why, but suddenly her youthful daydreams surfaced into excitement and elation.

'I'll go with you tonight if you'll come to the Tate Gallery with me tomorrow morning'.

'Tate Gallery? There's nothing for you there. Those arty types are unreliable, covered in hair, take dope, believe in free love and should be avoided,' warned Janet, a self-proclaimed woman of the world. 'You'll be kidnapped by a man with a beard, drugged, and forced to pose nude for all his friends.'

'Don't be silly – you sound just like Mummy, well, except for the rude bits, of course.' Doreen had an overwhelming curiosity to see what had always been forbidden to her. This was London Life – Life with a capital L. She suddenly regretted with all her heart lacking any artistic proclivities whatsoever.

The next morning, having found last night's soirée tiring and tiresome, Doreen awoke with a start, heart racing with excitement, but no amount of shaking could rouse Janet.

'Well, I can't miss this chance – maybe a once in a lifetime opportunity.'

She dressed hurriedly, noting from her tube map that the nearest underground station to the Tate Gallery was Pimlico...

It was a dazed but exhilarated Doreen who boarded a homebound train that evening, memories of the treasure trove of delights swirling in her head, and next day in her lunch hour she went, very timidly, to enrol for evening classes at the local college.

Her tutor, Mr Francesco, a bearded Bohemian with a limp, found such enthusiasm and raw talent in a plain young girl quite fascinating. 'You should take this up full-time – your brain is like a sponge soaking up new information. But first untie your lovely long hair, remove those glasses and wear some eye-makeup,' he advised. He bought her a duffel coat and contact lenses for Christmas and began calling her Dora.

Six months later, under the influence of Mr Francesco's persuasive powers, a bewildered Mr and Mrs Brighouse finally agreed to allow Doreen to give up the safe day job and return to full-time education, where it soon became apparent where her special genius lay.

Having originally been inspired by Rodin's The Kiss and Degas's Little Ballerina, Doreen decided to leave the human form to the Old Masters and, with Mr Francesco's assistance, concentrated instead on creating large sculptures of marble and stone, riddled with tiny holes, or, in other words, three-dimensional *pointillism.* This was a totally new idea.

Hailed as "the new Barbara Hepworth", Doreen went on to create her impression of a gigantic porous aquatic creature, entitled "Sponge" which, naturally, took the Art World by storm.

In her Carver Prize acceptance speech at the Guildhall, Doreen announced to the ecstatic audience that she was presently concentrating on a new work, her impression of a vast piece of Emmenthal, called simply "Cheese".

Finally, after the cheering had died down, she hastened to thank not only her bemused parents for their lifelong support and belief in her artistic abilities, but also her Svengali, her mentor, her beloved husband, Mr Francesco.

For, yes, dear reader – it was she – *the* Dora Francesco of recent legend – the most original, controversial and celebrated sculptress of the Twentieth Century.

BABY'S BREATH

When Stella our only child died giving birth, my dear wife Mary and I were overwhelmed by sorrow and joy all at the same time – a strange sensation. Some people might describe such a feeling as "poignant" and it sounds about right to me.

You see, we were consumed with love for our motherless granddaughter, Amelia, whom we looked after for our son-in-law David whilst he valiantly tried to keep working in spite of his terrible tragedy.

As time passed, David met an American girl at the office and pretty soon they married and went to live in New York State taking our beloved Amelia with them. David's new wife seemed a good and caring woman. They promised to keep in touch and I am sure they meant it when they said it, but still Amelia's goodbye baby-breath kiss had left salt-water on my cheek.

Of course, Mary and I felt bereaved for a second time in the space of eighteen months, and my poor dear wife never seemed to recover her usual lively spirits after that.

We did not have a large circle of friends to compensate for our lack of family, but Mary and I were self-sufficient, normally content in each other's company and we would sit in the evenings by the fire, drinking our tea, listening to the wireless, she endlessly knitting baby things while I smoked my pipe. It always seemed to be winter.

And it was a particularly hard winter when Mary fell ill. Snow lay on the ground for weeks and long sharp icicles hung from the gutters like so many stalactites. I had to call the doctor one morning and

Mary was taken away in an ambulance. After another seven days when the icicles had still not begun to thaw, I went round breaking them off before they did someone an injury. That was the evening they brought me the sad news.

Naturally, I gave Mary a good send-off in an oak coffin smothered in a cloud of pink and white Gypsofila – her favourite flower which she always referred to as Baby's Breath. My next-door neighbours, Ron and Ethel Longroyd, came to support me at the graveside bringing a wreath, which I did appreciate, although I didn't put my gratitude into words for some reason.

They came back here following the low-key funeral and, after they had witnessed my home-made Last Will and Testament, I gave them a cup of tea and a biscuit. I didn't have the heart to cater properly for mourners. But I am only a man so I probably got away with it.

'Look here, Frank – you'll always let us know if you need help, won't you,' Ethel said kindly, her moist eyes crinkling at the corners, 'or even a bit of companionship. Don't sit in here all by yourself, you know.'

'I'll be all right, Ethel,' I replied, wanting to say more but, as a man of few words, left it there. I hope it wasn't too abrupt.

After that I became a bit of a recluse, staying indoors with the curtains closed and only venturing out the once when my stock of tobacco and porridge ran low.

Mr Rahman at the corner shop agreed to deliver once a fortnight to save me the trouble. I gave him a key and he would leave a bag of groceries inside the shuttered back porch without disturbing me. I always left him a cheque in payment together with a new shopping list. He also settled the occasional bill for me. This arrangement worked well.

Ron and Ethel called round two or three times but I didn't go to the door; I peeped through a chink in the curtains then quickly dodged back although I'm afraid they probably did see me. They rang the bell and knocked for such a long time, but then I heard their footsteps moving away and the front gate clanged shut.

Cleanliness was once a priority in this house, but the gaunt face now reflected back in the grimy mirror over the mantel was barely recognisable, although my beard did not grow beyond a grizzled stubble. I was aware that my knitted cardigan was stiff with blobs of dried porridge and decorated with shreds of tobacco and grey ash.

And my body-clock was obviously confused, my circadian rhythm shot to pieces. I knew not whether it was day or night, neither sunlight nor moonbeams ever being allowed to penetrate the heavy velvet-draped windows. I had forgotten how beautiful the daytime could be, and how mysterious the night: these things ceased to matter.

I stopped going upstairs to bed, preferring to doze in my usual chair by the fireplace, so many dead embers now turned to dust in the grate. It must have been summer then, for I never felt cold.

How long I existed in this fashion, from hour to hour, day to day, week to week, I do not know. It could have been a short time or it could have been years.

I remember once snapping out of this dreamlike state, suddenly, in the bleak kitchen. I was stirring my porridge in the black encrusted pan on the stove when a sudden disturbance in the air at my shoulder, like a warm breath on my cheek, made me turn: out of the corner of my eye I saw, or rather sensed, a movement, a presence disappearing into the hall.

It must be this weak light playing tricks with my poor old eyes, I thought, intending to rootle under the stairs in the glory hole to find a replacement light bulb.

Unless the house is haunted, I laughed to myself, or I'm seeing things. Yes, that's most likely it – hallucinations. After all, I've never really believed in ghosts although I have been afraid of them all my life!

But strangely enough, my brain felt clearer than for many a day.

I went and sat in my chair by the hearth and began spooning grey porridge into my mouth, when I gradually became aware of a diffused light in the hall seeming to emanate from the double doors of the dining room which I had not entered since Mary's funeral.

What's this – burglars? I wondered, half rising from my chair. Then the light disappeared and I sat down again with a thud. 'Pull yourself together, lad,' I said aloud as my porridge bowl fell with a clatter into the stone hearth.

I calmed down and, as usual, dozed off listening to the wireless, probably the Home Service, or it may have been the World Service, I couldn't be sure which.

Suddenly, I awoke with a start, my neck in a crick. What was that noise? It wasn't the radio – it came from the hall. Voices – indistinct, but definitely voices. The fluting tones of a woman, a baby's chuckle, the rumbling tenor of a man.

I switched the wireless off and, trembling with fear, crept to the partly-open hall door and sidled through. But what was going on? Who were these people? How had they got into the house? There was a young woman with a baby, strangely familiar to me, and a man with a clipboard.

Could it be Stella, my beautiful daughter, holding baby Amelia in her arms. How was that possible? Could they be spirits, ghosts, shades? Oh God, no – had Amelia died in America and joined her mother in the afterlife?

But the baby was looking straight at me – she could see me, she smiled and reached out her little hand as I moved forward, and I felt her breath on my raddled old cheek. Oh Amelia, baby Amelia! Then the voices began again and I strained to hear their words.

I could not quite catch...

Ah, now I could hear... The young woman was speaking in an American accent to the man. 'Yes, Mr Beasley, it is very sad. The shopkeeper found my grandfather in his chair. He'd died of hypothermia. Too awful to contemplate! And I'll always be thankful he left me the house, although it does need a whole bunch of repairs.'

Mr Beasley was nodding in sympathy. 'Will you keep it or sell it on after the renovations?'

'Oh, I'll keep it now we're back in the UK. My husband loves the house, says it has good vibes. We'll be able to give it some real tender loving care, and anyway my late mother lived here as a girl which puts me right back in the bosom of my family.' The woman laughed self-consciously, and thought for a moment, hugging her baby. 'You know, I never saw my grandparents again after we went to the States. I was less than two years old at the time so I don't remember them at all. But I've named my daughter in their honour: Frances Mary – Frankie for short, although we often call her Baby's Breath in fun – I have no idea why.'

GHOST WRITER

The time is three o'clock of a November afternoon. I have finished writing my Magnum Opus and shall sit here for a while by the window staring into the swirling grey fog outside, gathering my courage before acting upon my final instructions which arrived this morning.

Dear friends, you may be wondering how I came to this sorry state? Then kindly allow me to relate my tale to you; it happened in this wise.

I had taken a week's leave from my tidy desk in the busy insurance office of J Pegram (Bristol), where I had been employed for thirty years. I had a secure position as Chief Clerk, having first been hired as a messenger boy at the age of thirteen.

Being neither married nor promised, and, leading as I did a solitary existence, I would invariably decline to take my holiday entitlement, preferring instead to attend to my work each day but, for once, I felt the need of a rest and a change of scene.

Leaving my austere Clifton apartment in the safekeeping of Mrs Goodbody, the landlady, I betook myself by omnibus to Bath where I had booked into a guest house for five days upon the recommendation of my immediate superior, Mr Beanstock, a kind man who had insisted I indulged in a respite for the good of my nerves.

As soon as I had taken occupation of a pleasant suite of rooms in Quiet Street, I decided to explore my environs before dusk, politely refusing a late luncheon offered by the proprietress.

As you will know, Bath has many winding lanes and alleys, full to bursting with small shops of character selling all manner of goods. I strolled along, glancing this way and that, noting the rich array of stylish apparel and jewellery, and feasting my eyes in the windows of patissiers, chocolatiers and similarly exotic confectioners.

Being abstemious, if not ascetic, I resisted any temptation to spend my hard-earned money on these luxury items, and walked on before coming to a sudden halt outside a second-hand shop. The sign over the door proclaimed "Z. Lazarus – Antiques" and, on a whim, I decided to go in, although I had never before experienced an interest in such matters.

Stooping slightly to avoid the low lintel, I entered the gloomy interior where my eyes gradually discerned a jumble of furniture of every description plus bedding, bicycles, toys, perambulators, fire irons, mounds of clothing, old boots and worn-down shoes. It was a veritable Aladdin's cave of detritus.

I began to browse, picking up and dropping items indiscriminately, with some distaste, until I became aware of a slight movement behind a curtained recess at the back of the shop, from whence I beheld a wizened figure loping towards me. He was dressed in rags and, incongruously, sported a colourful bejewelled smoking cap.

'Good afternoon, sir, and how can I help you in your search for the perfect gift?' he queried, one finger pressed to a wispy chin. 'I have here a marvellous elephant's foot umbrella stand just come in today which would suit a gentleman's lifestyle; and for your good lady wife (pardon my presumption), an embroidered firescreen to protect her delicate complexion of a winter's evening; or, no obligation, please try on this pair of riding boots (I apologise for the mud, by the way) which look to be just about your size, give or take. No, no, I can see you're not keen. Hmm.'

'I'm so sorry, Mr er, Lazarus,' I replied, 'You are most civil, but I was simply looking, that is all.'

But then my eye lit upon a most interesting item, a Blickensderfer 5, the first portable typewriter, a collector's item, one would imagine; I gazed upon it mesmerised, touching its dusty keys with gentle fingertips.

'Yes, I can see you're interested in this fascinating piece of machinery, known as The Five Pound Office in its day. It belonged to a famous author, if I'm not mistaken.'

'Oh? Which writer was that?' Could this be enthusiasm beginning to stir within me?

'Unfortunately, I cannot quite bring the name to mind, but I believe he worked himself to death, burning the midnight oil, they say. Hmm, a dead artist is more valuable than a living one, methinks, heh heh; it was true in his case, at any rate. If only I could recall… hmm?'

'I have heard it of painters, but it could refer to writers too,' I replied, bemused. 'I'll take it, if you please. What is the cost?'

'Hmm, it's in good working condition but you can have it cheap because ribbons may be hard to come by for such an ancient model, so I've been told. You can have it for ten shillings – no offers.'

What a bargain at the price, I thought, carrying the precious burden back to my rooms in Quiet Street.

The remainder of my stay passed pleasantly enough but I was impatient to begin pressing those keys, to see my words appearing on virginal white foolscap paper. What prose would issue forth, I had as yet no idea.

When I returned to Clifton, Mrs Goodbody met me at the door. 'Mr Peregrine,' said she, "welcome home. Here is a package which arrived by carrier this morning,' and she handed me a largish parcel.

How exciting, I thought, wondering who could have sent me a present, there being no return address visible.

Before even unpacking or changing my travelling coat for the usual velvet smoking jacket, I undid the string and sealing wax, removing layers of brown wrapping with trembling fingers.

Inside was a ream of white foolscap paper together with a replacement ribbon for the Blickensderfer 5. I immediately thought of Mr Lazarus, although I had not given him my personal details.

And then a handwritten note came fluttering onto the carpet, which read: 'You are destined to create a literary masterpiece: your Magnum Opus in five volumes, which will be written in secret. When it is finished, only then will you receive instructions regarding your final action. Believe this - you will become the most famous author in the world.'

Who could have resisted such a promise, a transformation of one's increasingly pointless life? I began to write, each and every evening into the small hours, barely eating or sleeping, and thus turning up at the office half-awake, unfit for work.

After several weeks, and remaining silent in the face of Mr Beanstock's entreaties, I made an irreversible mistake on a maturing policy, paying out hundreds of pounds too much to a policy-holder.

Of course, I was dismissed on the spot. But I did not care, and cleared out my desk with alacrity, rushing with all speed back to my apartment, heart bursting with joy as I sat down once more at the Blickensderfer 5 and, connecting with my muse, began to press the keys.

After that, I dedicated myself to writing the Magnum Opus, all day, every evening and most of the night, stopping occasionally to eat a little of the food left in the inner hall by a concerned Mrs Goodbody. She called through the door once or twice, asking whether a doctor should be fetched, but I reassured her things were fine and I was happy, happier than I had ever been.

Each weekend, a parcel would arrive with yet more stationery and typewriter ribbons, plus, after I lost my employment, a quantity of banknotes, which more than paid for my board and lodging.

The manuscript grew, quickly stacking up in box files against the wall. My prose needed no editing, nor any corrections, as I churned out the foolscap sheets like one possessed.

I must have stayed in my chambers for three years, totally dedicated to the Magnum Opus. I once heard Mrs Goodbody describe me as an eccentric recluse to a caller in the outer hallway, mayhap it was Mr Beanstock, but I knew not who and did not care.

Occasionally catching sight of my reflection in the looking-glass, I hardly recognised the scrawny, unkempt, hollow-eyed man staring back. That is a real starving artist, I laughed to myself, rubbing at another stain on my velvet jacket, before returning joyfully to my writing, and when the manuscript reached half a million words, my task came to a natural conclusion. The Magnum Opus was finished.

And now, here I sit by the window, glancing across intermittently at a thick loop of rope swinging from a hook in the ceiling.

The noose, yes, the noose – for that is what it is – arrived by parcel post this morning, and I recalled Mr

Lazarus's words: "A dead artist is more valuable than a living one, methinks."

It was then I knew what I had to do.

Dear friends, you may say I was misled from the start but, being a man of my word, I must carry out my instructions, the final part of the bargain, in the cause of celebrity – of my posthumous fame.

BUZZ!

Like the Queen, I never carry money, although I did once see a documentary where HM handed over half-a-crown in a Sandringham estate shop for some confectionery. What they probably mean by the Queen never carrying money is that she doesn't need to keep large amounts of cash upon her person as her every requirement is already catered for. I once read that HM had never travelled on a bus and was ignorant of the fact that some houses didn't have bathrooms...

But I digress! So I'll get to my point – which is shopping! I admit I quite like shopping, yes, you might say that. I could indulge my retail therapy eight days a week but have to be content with seven, and even on Christmas Day I go out on the prowl and invariably find a corner shop open, very useful for laying in a stock of tinned cling peaches, provided the proprietor is agreeable to accepting payment by credit card. Buying goods and carrying them home, that's my buzz, and I go on my way rejoicing.

But normally I'll avoid the little local shops and get on the number 34 bus after 9 a m, courtesy of my Senior Travelcard, and ride down to town each and every morning, returning home absolutely laden. If I'm attracted to something, I'll buy it. Be it clothes, shoes, accessories, biscuits, makeup, toiletries, lamps, clocks, watches, jewellery, anything – I have to own these things: that's my buzz.

Two bedrooms of the house are given over to my purchases which are stacked to the ceilings, box upon box. I keep a detailed account of every item plus a code number which tells me where it's stored in case I need to inspect it, because I never wear any of the garments or other adornments, neither do I eat any of the biscuits and sweets, nor do I use the lamps, clocks and toiletries, nor do I carry any of the designer handbags around. Owning them is an end in itself, proprietorship is all: something like being a stamp collector or a lover of ceramics or a connoisseur of fine art. I imagine this is the reason famous works by the Old Masters are cut out of their frames and stolen – certain people will pay a high price for a painting just for the pleasure of owning a work of beauty, for the thrill of feasting their eyes on such an object in private: that's their buzz.

Occasionally I will do a little shoplifting, only small items though, as I do know right from wrong. It's quite easy when you know how, and the danger of it provides a more intense buzz on an otherwise ordinary shopping day.

No-one knows about my acquisitiveness, my passion for possessions. It's my secret, my buzz. As previously mentioned, my purchases are paid for at the point of sale by one of my credit cards and each month I will rob Peter to pay Paul, although I have to say that my debts have increased rather alarmingly in spite of recently taking out yet another equity release on the house. This had the desired effect of making me feel more secure for a while but now I see that my liabilities are mounting up again.

But what the hell! It's my hobby, my pastime – I don't go on expensive holidays, I don't smoke or drink. All I do is shop. Is that so terrible? Is it a crime to love buying things? I can't see that it hurts anyone else; it's *my* buzz.

Most of the clothes and shoes I collect are quite fashionable, or they are when I acquire them. After a few years some of them begin to look rather dated but I still like keeping them to look at, all safely sealed against dust and moisture in their plastic covers. I spend a fortune on those protective bags, and I mean the professional version, none of your supermarket mass-produced type of thing.

I was trawling through the boxes and shelves in the front bedroom this morning and couldn't help laughing at the swimsuits and beach wear, brightly-coloured towels, bottles of Scotch, jumbo packs of cigarettes. Anyone would think I was a jet-setter!

But even though I have no use for any of these things, I like having them around. In fact, this particular cotton sarong I'm thinking of comes in seven different shades, and I have one of each, plus, of course, matching thongs.

Yes, I do enjoy my hobby, probably a bit too much, because recently I have taken to going out to the shops again in the afternoons.

Really and truly, I should have tried to keep it to one excursion per day as my irresistible compulsion has had the effect of doubling my debts over a very short period of time. It seems I am now in the red to the tune of £100,000.

And it was only today when it suddenly dawned on me that I have this huge problem. I've been an ostrich for far too long. The thing I must do is attempt to extricate myself from it, get free of this bind, escape from this imbroglio. What to do? I need to make a lot of money very quickly.

I can't sell any of my stuff because I wouldn't know where to begin – eBay is way beyond my capabilities. The small ads or a car boot sale would never recoup even a small percentage of what I've paid out and might possibly attract the wrong kind of buyer. And anyway I am very attached to my collection – I don't really want anyone else to have it.

When I first started my hobby, it was a gradual, almost imperceptible course of events, an opportunistic process, but if I were able to begin again from scratch it could be with a definite goal, a more structured feel to the proceedings. Think of that thrill – setting out once more with nothing and slowly building it up. I could formulate a system of different categories and go out each day with a particular target in mind. Yes, that would certainly be a new kind of buzz.

Of course, it would be logical to start again from the ground up, I see that now. And I cherish my precious things so much that I would prefer to destroy the whole lot rather than have anyone else poking their noses in, handling them or, lord forbid, actually wearing or using any item whatsoever out of my collection.

I've been thinking about it, churning it over in my mind for the past hour, and I know it would solve all my financial worries. So, to cut a long story short, I've been out shopping just now for the third time today, but it was only to Petherville's Garage at the end of the road. I bought a can of petrol and a new lighter – I simply couldn't resist another lighter although I have fifty-three assorted ones upstairs.

Well, as I say – that's my buzz!

TO BE PERFECTLY HONEST

Hello, there! It's Mrs, er, isn't it? Room 15? Yes, I thought so; I saw you arrive yesterday. How are you liking it so far? Settling in OK? It's an absolute tragedy we have to come out here for a smoke though; what a stupid rule.

But anyway, I hope Matron has warned you about certain persons. For instance, the lady in Room 42, Mrs oh, something-or-other – um, can't remember her first name either, to be honest, and, quite frankly, I prefer not to be on first-name terms with the people in here.

Well, as I was saying, the woman in Room 42, yes, she's very uppity and walks with one of those Alzheimer things – oh, what's that? Yes, a Zimmer, that's right – well, that's what I said, one of those things you walk around with. She poles about like the Queen Mary does Mrs, oh – Her Ladyship, I call her, all that powder and rouge, and dripping with jewellery! Lord, she wears these great big glittering brooches on her chest, and rings on every finger and on her toes too, I shouldn't be surprised. Next news, she'll have one through her nose except she's a bit long in the tooth to get away with that sort of thing and she could get an infection from the, oh you know, the whatnot you sew with, yes, needle, that's it.

And you know how chilly it was last night? Well, apparently Mrs, er, thing, Her Ladyship, rang the, tinkle tinkle, yes, that's right, the bell and asked them to put a bidet on her bed. A bidet! I ask you. Of course she meant a – a – a duvet, yes, that's right. They put a duvet on the bed, and then of course she complained of being too hot.

Well, she will wear nylon nighties. I keep telling her not to wear man-made fibres but she just gets annoyed and fobs you off. 'No, I prefer nylon,' she goes, 'it's easy to wash and it doesn't need, erm, you know one of those pointed gadgets you flatten things out with – yes, yes, an iron, ironing, that's it, and anyway I'm not senile.' So we're no further on.

And of course, she doesn't even have to do her own washing in here, the daft old bat. I don't have any sympathy with her, if I'm being perfectly honest with you; she's such a snob with her airs and graces, always trying to be so-o-o genteel but – I've never heard her say she's met the Royals.

Speaking of which, I must tell you about the time the Queen Mother very graciously got me a chair when I was pregnant and about to faint. Yes, really! The dear QM noticed me standing in the line waiting to be introduced and ordered a flunky to fetch me a chair PDQ, although she didn't say PDQ of course, the QM was *far too* well bred to use common language like that...

You know, I take my cue from the Queen Mother in *all things* – I cross my ankles in a ladylike manner when sitting (the QM was noted for that) and she *never* perspired, not even doing the Gay Gordons, so it's said. I'm not sure I can *always* aspire to not perspire but I do my best in that department and spend an absolute fortune on under-arm deodorant. And I'm told her husband, the old king, was a smoker, which is why I still enjoy my fags. So what I think is, if it's good enough for the Royals... well, what's sauce for the goosey gander, you know?

And oh, it was so funny this morning in the lounge, the TV repairman came to tune the television. He told me his name, it was, er, oh I've forgotten it now, but anyway, he had one of those things on his back, you know, a wadderyoucallit, no, not a monkey – no, it's one of those lumpy things that stick out and get in the way, no, no, silly, not a hump, he's not a hunchback. Oh, you know, yes, that's it, a knapsack, that was it. Well this chap was telling me all about his prostrate trouble, poor devil, so I told him all about my, you know, when I had all taken away, the up and under business – that! Yes, mysterectomy, that's it. We had a really long chat. Nice bloke, he is – has to wear those electricated stockings apparently, otherwise his legs swell up something shocking. I'm sure he was wearing makeup.

What was I telling you? I'm losing my, you know, erm, that other thing you sew with – no, not cotton – yes, thread. I'm losing my thread. Oh, that was it, Her Ladyship, in Room 42. *She* must have memory-loss because she will keep asking what day it is, and what's the time. Over and over. *And* there's a huge clock on the dining room wall. She must have bad eyesight if she can't see that. I'm short-sighted but I can see the clock all right. 'What's the time,' she says to no-one in particular, and 'What did I have for breakfast? Was it good? Did I eat it all up? Have I had my bath today?' Over and over. It's so *boring*. My advice is just ignore her, if I'm being perfectly honest with you.

Then last Tuesday, it was so funny at teatime – Her Ladyship sits at a table on her own, you know, probably because she's too grand to sit with the common herd. Anyway, she suddenly started laughing. Everyone stopped eating and looked up; she was watching herself in the mirror, roaring her head off, in stitches she was, so the whole room waited 'til she'd finished and then carried on with their meal, beans on toast we were having, if I remember correctly. But it was quite embarrassing, to be perfectly honest with you, because she's such an uppity woman, and she didn't seem to think anything of it so nobody said a word. You know, I'm sure most of them in here are batty – present company excepted, of course.

Now, what was I saying?

Oh, yes, having to come out here for a smoke – it's an utter disgrace. Anyway, I enjoyed our little chat, but no peace for the wicked, duty calls, and Mrs whatnot in Room 6 will be waiting for her insulin jab. Hmm, does this uniform look too tight? I really should go on a diet, to be perfectly honest.

SLEEPING PARTNERS

Edith Oakshott picked up one of her husband's socks from the workbasket and began, with swollen but deft fingers, to darn it with a length of matching wool. She knew what people would say if they could see her: It's the 1970s, Edith – no-one darns socks these days – just go out and buy Edward another pair at Marks & Sparks.

But Edith had always darned socks, ever since her marriage just after the war – make do and mend, they used to say, and she could not embrace the modern throwaway society. Inbuilt obsolescence is what it was. Cheap and cheerful was not for her and Edward – they preferred quality every time.

Similarly, Edith made her own bread and cakes, her own preserves, pickles, soups and sauces. Everything was made from scratch, even to growing her own vegetables in the back garden. To be truthful, she knew that Edward would be outraged if she started presenting him with shop-bought food. It didn't take much to put him in a black mood and over the years she had learnt to take the line of least resistance – anything for a quiet life.

'I blame you for this, you know,' was Edward's usual cry when anything had "gone awkward", as he termed it, from his irritation with the late arrival of the morning papers to more serious or important matters like tax demands.

Obviously, the courtship had not been a love match: Edward Oakshott had been bought for Edith by her father, Mr Corbishley, who wanted someone to take over the family brass foundry when he retired. Mr Corbishley considered the young man who was already a senior accountant in the firm to be an intelligent chap, just the right material for the job, whilst his daughter, a mere girl, was never considered bright enough for the role.

After renaming the company Corbishley & Oakshott, Edith's father promptly died.

There were two children of the Oakshotts' marriage – a girl Susan, and then, twelve months later, their son Nigel. After that, Edward moved out of the master bedroom into the guest room and so no more babies were forthcoming.

The children were a rich source of irritation to Edward. He complained bitterly about the noise they made, about the smell, a toy left on the carpet, if they caught a cold, the cost of schooling, how they performed in exams.

In turn, the children lived in awe of their father. Mealtimes were occasions of uneasy silences in spite of the wholesome home-cooked food served. Susan and Nigel waited to be addressed and only spoke when spoken to. 'Children should be seen and not heard,' their father would intone if one of them chanced to look askance during a meal or, heaven forbid, giggle nervously.

Edward blamed their mother for mollycoddling them when they cried, and on school holidays he took them for long hikes across rough terrain. No-one was allowed to watch the television apart from each Sunday evening when the family would be ordered to gather around for Songs of Praise although Edward was not at all religious.

Edith had these memories going through her mind as she continued darning his socks. She knew Edward resented the fact he owed his position in life to their marriage, which was the reason she had perforce remained a sleeping partner in the brass foundry although the company had been bequeathed to them jointly. Even so, they should have had a good life together, Edward and Edith, with their two lovely children, but it was not to be. 'Are you sure they're mine?' Edward would grumble. 'They don't look at all like me and they're not very bright either.'

It was no surprise to their mother when both Nigel and Susan dropped out of school. Nigel grew his hair into ringlets and took to wearing dresses and makeup; Susan shaved her head and wore dungarees. Edith accepted their life-choices philosophically, her only regret being that she would never be able to look forward to having grandchildren.

But Edward had grown apoplectic at each new craze in his offspring's development and the children began to refer to him as "the ranting man". In due course, there was a violent confrontation which resulted in Edward suffering a severe heart attack and a quietly tearful Edith waving goodbye to her offspring as they left to backpack round India. 'This is all your doing,' her husband would often pronounce, purple in the face, as he gulped down his essential blood-thinning drugs.

Edith said nothing – but her life was empty after the children had gone and she took solace in the continual round of household duties, obsessively cleaning the gloomy house from top to bottom until her finger-ends bled in the cold weather. She had never been allowed any domestic help, for Edward possessed a mean streak in addition to his other unattractive traits.

She finished darning the sock and decided to check on her husband who had gone to bed early with a heavy chest cold after leaving instructions for her to rouse him when it was time for his heart pills. She went upstairs and tapped on his bedroom door. There was no reply so she entered the room quietly. Edward was lying on his back, snoring loudly, in a deep sleep.

'If I disturb him he'll only be angry even though he told me to wake him up, so perhaps I'll leave him be,' she thought, taking the glass of water and medication back to the bathroom.

Edith returned to her workbasket and picked up another sock. She took her time over it, working the wool with her needle, warp and weft, into a neat woven patch. When it was finished, she thought she ought to check on Edward but changed her mind in case he shouted at her, and went to bed instead.

The next morning, bright and early, Edith went straight downstairs; lovingly she tended her vegetable patch, then did some baking, and at lunchtime stopped for a bowl of home-made soup and a roll. In the afternoon she scrubbed the kitchen floor, and in the evening took up her needlework and, as a special treat, watched Coronation Street before falling asleep in her chair.

And so it went, days and nights of staying downstairs, pleasing herself, playing the waiting game.

When it was almost bedtime on the fourth evening, she thought it might be advisable to look in on Edward and climbed the casement, up the floral-patterned stair-carpet, holding onto the brown handrail with one hand and the decorative wallpaper border, also in brown, with the other. She did not bother to knock but entered the bedroom where Edward was still on his back, but instead of snoring, the sound of death rattled in his throat.

'Well now, what shall I wear,' she wondered. She had heard that, unless you happened to be royalty, deep black was not absolutely necessary these days, which was all to the good as it meant not having to spend a fortune on new clothes: old habits die hard. She went to her own bedroom and looked through the wardrobe, taking out a coat in black and white houndstooth check bought ten years ago from Marks's. 'This has been a dependable little coat, and so versatile,' she said to herself. 'I could wear it with a black scarf tied in a floppy bow at the neck and maybe a black beret on my head, but it might be better to just wear a black velvet headband – there's bound to be one in Nigel's dressing table drawer, I'm almost certain.'

It took quite a while sorting through her drab collection of garments and accessories. After selecting a short charcoal grey skirt, years out of date, she suddenly stopped and decided to look in on Edward again. He was lying in the same position as before, but silently, his face grey in death, one eye partly open.

Edith nodded to herself, heaved a sigh, and knew what she had to do. After painting a wide smile on the dead man's mouth with one of Nigel's tangerine lipsticks left behind when he took off for India, she went downstairs and fetched her workbasket.

'Perhaps a glittery georgette scarf would liven up the proceedings,' she suggested to the deceased, settling herself in the basket chair by his bed. 'Black - it must be black, though, don't you agree, but with beads and sequins. I do love how they sparkle and catch the light, although I've never been allowed to wear such things before. Oh, and if you're wondering, I'll just tell the doctor that you refused to take your heart pills – he'll believe me, he knows what a stubborn pig you are – I mean, were.'

Smiling serenely, she picked up a white shirt of Edward's that needed attention. 'I'll turn this collar and it'll be like new – you can wear it in your coffin,' she said, nodding pleasantly at her sleeping partner, and enjoying for the first time in her married life a companionable silence.

ANGEL

Now, I do like Christmas! Christmas is cool, what with all the presents and stuff, and I get everything I want – usually. In fact Mummy goes a bit mad, a bit over the *top* with all the *shopping*. Daddy says she's a shopaholic – *she* says he's an *alcoholic*.

But – yuk, I hate it when people get me cardigans and pyjamas and stuff. *Stupid*! So bo-o-oring. If they get me a present, it should be *toys* – well, toys or video games, and books too, I expect.

And the Nativity Play, that I could do without - it's so bo-o-oring – and quite *stupid* and babyish, really. Last year they made me be the ox, but, oh no, the horns wouldn't stay put – they kept slipping over my eyes.

This time Miss Lippincott says I can be the Angel Gabriel, so that means the long white nightie and a pair of big glittery wings – and I'll get to wear some sparkly eye-makeup and lipstick. *Cool*!

But anything is better than being the ox – I was so embarrassed and got teased about it for weeks, especially by that stupid Rosie Pettifer – hmm! Actually, *she* should be made to be the ox – better still, the *donkey!*

Last year, Rosie was Holy Mary, but kept dropping Baby Jesus on his head – it was only a doll, though. Everyone laughed behind their hands but nobody teased her about it later in case she told her big brother and his gang. They're *disgusting* – they smoke behind the bike sheds, you know – *Ummm*!

This year Rosie's going to be one of the shepherds. She says she'd prefer to be the Angel – *Hello-o-o – I don't think so*! Luckily as a shepherd she'll be covered in a hood or a tea towel, probably.

Some People

And Rosie should *not* be going around telling everybody I'm the teacher's pet. I'm like – *Hello o-o - Rosie Pettifer –* I think you're *jealous!!!*

Cuz' Miss Lippincott says *I* look just right for the part as long as I remember to tell Mummy not to cut my hair before the actual day. It won't be difficult playing the angel – all I have to do is stand there with my arms out, not speaking.

Actually, *nobody* will have to speak! Miss Lippincott is going to be "narrator", which means she'll do all the talking this time. This is because of last year when Joseph got mixed up and began his lines all over again, and then they were all going round and round in a loop.

It **was** funny but *really* annoying! Mr Arbuthnot had to *shout out* the next line to that stupid Ben, I *mean* Joseph, to get him back on track otherwise we'd have been there all afternoon. *Pathetic!*

So I'm glad we have Miss Lippincott this year. I just hope it's not too bo-o-oring, being the Angel Gabriel! But anyway, after that, we break up for the Christmas Holidays and I won't have to look at Rosie Pettifer's freckled face for three whole weeks! Oh – *Wicked*!

CRUMBS

Mrs Stacey came in today for her weekly bacon and margarine. She still calls it her "rations" instead of groceries even though the war has been over for nearly seven years. 'Good morning, Missus! Your usual?' I said, removing my chewed cigar and placing it under the counter. 'Yes, and I'll have half a pound of broken biscuits while you're at it, oh, and a quarter of Peeko Tips,' she said.

No good-mornings from Mrs Stacey. Just because she wears a fur coat she thinks she's a cut above everybody else! Violet says it's most likely rabbit fur, if the truth were told, and Violet is usually right in most things, or she thinks she is and I let her think she is. I've learnt through long years of marriage how to take the line of least resistance in order to lead a fairly quiet life.

'Can I interest you in some of this special corned beef that's just arrived from the sultry shores of Argentina?' I asked Mrs Stacey, all friendly-like. 'It won't be in stock very long, I'm sure. I could put some aside for you, if you wish.'

'Oh, going begging, is it?' she said, breathing all over the tray of chocolate marshmallows with not one word of thanks for my courtesy and thoughtfulness. 'You're wasting your time trying to offload it on me – Reginald won't touch processed food, but I will take two currant teacakes while I'm here. And a jar of blackberry jam. That will do for our tea tonight.'

As I was slicing the bacon on the thinnest setting, Andrew came into the shop wheeling his delivery bike.

'Oi, take that round the back – I won't tell you again,' I said sharply to the young whippersnapper, then turning to Mrs Stacey, I gave a beaming smile. 'The youth of today!' I remarked pleasantly. She ignored me but glared Andrew up and down with a look of distaste.

'Aw, I can't, Mr Blackstock,' he squeaked in a voice not yet fully broken. 'Mrs Blackstock has locked the back gate and I can't get her to hear me for love nor money.'

'Oi, that's enough lip from you, young feller me lad,' I said, folding the bacon up in greaseproof paper. 'Just prop your bike up in the alleyway and then come back through and go open the gate yoursen. Mrs Blackstock is probably upstairs having a nap.'

Mrs Stacey sniffed. 'Hmm, it's all right for some, I'm sure' she said. 'Catch me having time to spare for a nap during the day. And when are you going to get some proper butter in – Reginald is sick of margarine. We've put up with it all through the war – I bet the *Germans* have butter – and *they* lost.'

I answered this with another beaming smile, nodded my head a few times in agreement and began to hum "The Bluebells of Scotland" softly to myself as I carried on preparing her order.

By the time I'd weighed out half a pound of broken biscuits and a quarter of Peeko Tips, I had quite a queue of one or two people in the shop. I totted up Mrs Stacey's bill. 'There we are, Missus! And I haven't charged you for the extra bit of bacon rind that was going begging. You'll have to run it under the tap though – it fell on the floor – won't do you any harm, I'm sure, those bits of sawdust. Now, that'll be two and sixpence ha'penny, if you please.'

'Hmm, two and sixpence ha'penny? It's daylight robbery if you ask me,' she said, turning to the customer standing behind her. 'I shall start going to town for my shopping if prices go up much more.'

The person standing behind her was Mrs Grindrod, a shabby female in a floral wrap-around housedress, her mousy hair escaping in thin wisps from a knitted turban. 'Yes, it's a downright scandal,' the Grindrod woman agreed, nodding her head, a cigarette dangling from a corner of her mouth. 'I don't know how we manage, these days. Me old man's always in the pub, always at the dog-track and always got a fag in his gob. How does the government expect us to feed the kids and pay for our small comforts, all at the same time?'

Mrs Stacey was obviously not pleased with the way the conversation was going, so she picked up her purchases, bundled them into a brown leather shopping bag, and swept out of the door with a flourish of her fur coat, tinkling the shop bell as she went.

'Well, Missus!' I said to the Grindrod woman, spreading my hands on the counter-top, 'what can I get you today? May I interest you in some special corned beef, arrived this very morning all the way from the exotic cattle ranches of Argentina?'

'Good God, no,' she replied, her cigarette stuck to her bottom lip. 'Argentina – I've heard of that – it's abroad, isn't it? We don't like any of that there foreign muck in our house. Alf likes his steak and kidney pie and chips and rice pudding – all good English food.'

'Is that right, Missus?' I retorted before I could stop myself. 'But have you ever wondered where the ingredients come from? For a start, the rice comes from China.'

'Ingredients? What you talking about? Our food hasn't got ingredients in it – I'm ever so careful about things like that. Now what I came in for was a large sliced loaf and a jar of strawberry jam. That'll do for the kids' tea and tomorrow's breakfast. Oh, and I'll have half a pound of broken biscuits and a bottle of Chop Sauce as well. And two ounces of satin cushions - yeh, and a quarter of those sherbet lemons – lor, me mouth's watering just thinking of 'em.'

She parted her lips in a winning smile displaying a set of jagged brown teeth, and her cigarette fell into the tray of chocolate marshmallows, burning a hole in one of them. 'Oh, sorry about that,' she snorted, picking up the cigarette and placing it back in her mouth.

'Oh, er, never mind, Missus!' I said, remembering that the customer is always right, and quickly removed the offending item of confectionery whilst silently planning to stick a glazed cherry over the hole – no-one would ever notice, and, if they did, I would deny all knowledge and blame the bakery.

Angela, our Saturday girl, turned up eventually – late, as usual. I've told her straight, she won't get a better boss than me if I give her the sack. But she just laughs in my face and I let her get away with it because she is a lovely girl, only in her teens, the same age as our Gillian would have been, had she lived.

Everyone loves Angela: young Andrew is mad about her (much to my disapproval) and even the wife likes her, and that's saying something. Violet will sometimes come through into the shop to have a chat with Angela, but usually she prefers staying in the back doing her knitting and sewing, listening to organ music and Mrs Dale's Diary on the Light Programme, and eating anything that's not nailed down.

'Now, Missus,' I said to Angela, 'these are your instructions for today. There's a cartload of corned beef to shift, so do your best. And if anyone asks for butter, just tell them I haven't had a delivery as yet and push the marge at them.'

'OK, Cedric,' said Angela. 'Just leave it to me.'

'Now, look here, Missus – don't be so familiar with your elders and betters. I've told you before and I won't tell you again.'

'Oh well, if you won't tell me again, I can keep on doing it then,' she giggled, commencing to clear up the mess from a bag of sugar that had split.

The afternoon was quite busy after that but by five o'clock I could see Angela was excited and eager to be off, so I told her she could go home early. 'Suit yourself, Cedric,' she grinned and was off like a rat up a drainpipe – going jiving at the Mecca Locarno with young Andrew, I expect. The cheeky little madam! She does put me in mind of our Gillian.

When the shutters eventually went up at six o'clock, I cleared away in a hurry, wiped the bacon-slicer down with the old dishcloth I keep under the counter, and hung up my striped apron behind the door. I just couldn't wait to go through into our private living quarters at the back.

'Violet, love,' I called out. 'Would you like a corned beef sandwich for tea? I managed to keep a few slices back. And, look what I've got – none of that old margarine for us tonight. I had a consignment of butter delivered this morning and I've kept it to one side specially for thee and me.'

'Cedric Blackstock,' said Violet emerging from the kitchen, eyes moist with emotion, wiping her hands on her pinafore. 'You're such a good lad, always coming up with these little treats,' and she gave me a smacker, full on the lips. Unfortunately, she had a mouthful of broken biscuits at the time, but, in spite of the crumbs, I was a happy man.

Oh, yes – I know which side my bread is buttered!

TWINGE

Mother woke me in the night complaining she had a twinge: it was in her leg this time. I brought her a painkiller and sat by the bed until she went back to sleep but then, of course, I felt like a wet rag this morning. So I left a message for Simon Blinkhorn, my second in command at the village library, to say I'd be taking the day off, and then I telephoned the surgery.

It was that useless Jackie Clack who answered. I related in depth the problem with Mother's leg, and asked what time could we expect Dr Frobisher to call. 'Mother, I mean, Mrs Gorringe, won't have anyone but Dr Frobisher,' I told her firmly.

'Yes,' she said, 'we are aware of your mother's requirements, but doctor has a full complement of patients to deal with today.'

'Don't give me that,' I said, 'you're reading from a script! Please inform Dr Frobisher that Miss Gorringe made the request – he'll come all right.' Then I slammed the telephone down and made a mental note to write one of my famous letters of complaint to the practice about the girl's lack of customer care skills, because that kind of attitude is simply not helpful!

I do realise Mother has a reputation for crying wolf when there's often nothing much wrong with her, but I have to admit to being secretly pleased if her real or imagined ailments give me an excuse to call the doctor out. It's when she sits there moaning about nothing in particular or wants to discuss the pointlessness of life in general that I lose patience.

But after all, I remind myself, she *is* a helpless old woman, virtually housebound, moving no further than the gate for some years, although I suspect she could run the four-minute mile in the event of fire, tempest, flood or plague, especially a plague of locusts as she cannot abide insects of any description.

However, Mother and I do agree on one thing; we love Dr Frobisher – he is so charming and has, I believe, a soft spot for me. I manage to see him regularly about one thing or another, usually on a Wednesday when the library closes early.

This week it was my left ear itching inside, it was most uncomfortable and I was prescribed drops. He is very kind, calls me Dorcas – not that I would allow such familiarity from anyone but him (my staff at Quagmire Library refer to me as Miss Gorringe); and he smiles quizzically, peering over his half-moons and tells me I'm one of the worried well. 'You are one of the worried well, Dorcas,' he says. Oh, he's such a sweet man – with his noble head, lovely grey hair and dapper bow tie. Next week I could go see him about one of my allergies or maybe this callous on my foot.

So, back to Mother's leg. I was sitting by the window waiting for the doctor to arrive when I saw someone with a mass of frizzy black hair wheeling a bicycle right across the middle of our lawn and propping it against the silver birch, scraping off large chunks of bark in the process. Of course I quickly realised it was that damned Nurse Wildgoose.

And then – and I could hardly believe my eyes – she fumbled in the top pocket of her grubby white dress (doesn't she ever wash it?), and lit the cigarette dangling in readiness from her lips. It must have been a hand-rolled cigarette because the end caught fire – I saw the flame quite distinctly. She knew I was watching her but continued smoking for a few seconds more.

When I opened the front door she was sucking a mint and fanning her breath, her sallow skin glistening with perspiration, and I noticed with distaste a piece of cigarette paper stuck to her lower lip with a spot of blood.

You know, I was brought up to be polite, and so, even though I was seething, I said calmly, 'we *were* expecting Dr Frobisher'.

'He's too busy for house calls today, Miss Gorringe,' she retorted, 'you'll have to put up with little me instead – won't I do?'

'Oh,' I said, 'I'm not sure that Mother, I mean Mrs Gorringe, will see anyone else and while I'm on the subject, please keep off the grass.'

'Oh really,' she said, 'I'm so sorry. Now what's up with the old girl? I may as well see her now I'm here – can't waste a journey – got to cost it out and write it up in my records, see! Time is money.'

I made a mental note to add an additional item in my official letter of complaint to the practice, not only about the Wildgoose creature's lack of PR skills but also her slovenly appearance, filthy habits and stale breath. My fingers were itching to put pen to paper.

Well, when Mother saw who had turned up, she nearly had a stroke. However, we Gorringes are well-known for having impeccable manners and so Mother allowed the Wildgoose creature to give her leg a cursory examination, with very rough hands, as she told me later, before whining that she felt very much better now, thank you, and was ready for her midday nap.

'That's right Mrs G, there's nothing much wrong with you – only old age, ahahaha. You could try moving about a bit more. That would help your circulation, I'm sure.'

My nerves twinged with irritation as I showed the Wildgoose creature out. She stopped in the porch, fumbling in her top pocket for the squashed, yellowing cigarette, and turning to me said in a confidential tone, 'Shall I book you in for your usual emergency appointment?'

'No,' I said stiffly, 'I can make my own arrangements, thank you.'

She laughed, gave a shrug, said 'Suit yourself' and trudged across the lawn to her bicycle which she wheeled back towards the gate leaving yet more tyre marks on our neat lawn.

Really, the impertinence of that creature! What is she implying – that I'm riddled with disease? I'm as fit as a fiddle – Dr Frobisher says so: 'Dorcas,' he says, 'you are one of the worried well.'

He tells me that every week – so it must be true!

DRAWN

There had been a framed colour-washed sketch of a jam-jar full of bluebells standing on a rotting tree-trunk. It had hung on the cellar wall for as long as anyone could remember. I would listen, rapt, as my grandmother recounted, yet again, how her Great Aunt Peg had sketched it sitting in a copse above a valley somewhere in the Yorkshire Dales. Family legend had it that this very work of art had won some sort of a nationwide art competition, and Peg had been obliged to travel all the way to London for the day to receive her prize, the sum of ten shillings.

Great Aunt Peg must have presented an eccentric figure, especially in those days at the turn of the twentieth century. She wore men's clothes, a flat cloth cap and smoked a clay pipe; she never married in spite of receiving many proposals from similarly attired gents who may have discerned their own image reflected back, something like Narcissus only different. But Peg continued to exercise her feminine side which included executing delicate works of art.

In summer, the front step of the Victorian Gothic house was where she would sit, puffing on her pipe, cloth cap over her eyes, partly as a sunshade but mainly to avoid having to speak to any neighbour who deigned to pass too close to the wrought iron railings enclosing her scrubby little garden.

In winter, Peg would descend the steep casement to the huge dank cellar running under the length and breadth of the house, set up her easel and stay there all day, drawing sketch after sketch in front of the banked-up coal fire in the black-leaded hearth.

There was a blurred grey photograph of Peg which my grandmother, if cajoled, would take out and display. When grandma died, I was left the snap in a box of other family photographs. What a treasure trove! The prize-winning artwork of the jam-jar of bluebells was also my grandmother's legacy to me, but, now yellowing, it was left hanging on the whitewashed wall down in the cellar, which had, after all, been Peg's workspace. It would have seemed a sacrilege to take it down.

How things change! Years later, during World War II, those wrought iron railings were ripped out to make munitions, and that same cellar had been steel-lined and bomb-proofed for use as an air-raid shelter and many were the nights that our whole extended family would congregate in its comforting embrace. I would lie on the big bed in the warm subterranean womb with my little cousins and stare at Peg's framed still-life, wishing I could be in that copse with the bluebells far away from the whining of aircraft overhead.

In the fullness of time, I left home, and my parents eventually sold the house which had been in our family for over eighty years. A long time after we had all moved away, I thought of the colourwash sketch and wondered whether it was still there hanging on the wall in that damp cellar. I felt strangely drawn, until it became an obsession. It was mine, my legacy; after all, it had been left to me and no-one else. I began to have strange and worrying dreams at night, and knew I would have to go and find out for myself.

I hadn't told anyone about the sentimental journey I proposed to make today; the family consider me quite neurotic about my old home, and anyway everyone is away all week, so no-one would miss me for a few days. I was grateful for that this morning when setting off for the station where I bought an open return ticket, as I had no idea how my adventure would develop.

My head was in a whirl on the train. I was going through the motions of reading The Times, but my mind kept wandering, hoping my pilgrimage wouldn't turn out to be a wild goose chase; what if the house had been demolished after all? However, assuming it was still standing, it would be bound to look different after so many years and how I would gain access was pushed to the back of my mind.

Oh, the nostalgia of it all. It would be wonderful to see my old home once more, the house where I was born.

And what a bonus it would be if Great Aunt Peg's picture still hung in its place on the cellar wall.

The journey flew by and I was thrilled to arrive at City Station. I took a taxi to my old neighbourhood and it was sadly apparent that a lot of these old streets had already been pulled down, but then, there we were in Gas Street – still standing but boarded up, waiting for the bulldozer. Thank goodness I made it in time. Just look at my wonderful old home – it's so beautiful, can't everyone see that?

Quickly paying the bemused taxi driver who didn't speak much English anyway, I picked my way through the back yard of number 54 to the door which seemed to be missing its boarding and also a hinge, so it was fairly easy to squeeze myself inside. And, yes, there was the kitchen on the right with the deep Belfast sink. Mmm, the same nostalgic odour of damp stone. One step up to the living room door, there on my left. But I was drawn to the cellar, and here was the bomb-proof door, stiff and creaky but still solid, opening onto the familiar, dank casement stairs. Quick, where was the light-switch: drat, of course the electricity had been disconnected. I reached into my handbag, scrabbling for the box of matches, thankful for once I was a smoker – yes, that was better. Now I could see the cold slab halfway down where Mam used to put meat, margarine and butter, long before ordinary working people had fridges. Then I was down at the bottom of the staircase, and looking around – yes, this place really is vast: there's the sink, the copper and the rusty old range with its bread-oven. No furniture or rubbish down here now. Nothing left at all, no old tools, no ancient bed. But there is still a dusty old frame on the wall, and in it – yes, Peg's still-life, almost unrecognisable through the grim grime of years.

And there I was still staring unbelievingly at the picture frame, trying to reach on tiptoe, when I heard an awful noise! What was that crash? The cellar door had slammed! Help! I ran back up the stone steps. Oh, no – it had jammed solid! My God, I couldn't budge it!

And now my fingernails were broken, they were bleeding. Dear Lord, this is a terrible place – no-one will hear me down here.

Oh, by all that's holy, I shall wake up in a moment, of course I will, oh please let me! Hail Mary full of grace, the Lord is with thee, blessed art thou – I'm sorry – I promise you, my Holy Mother in Heaven, I'll go to church – I should have listened. Why was I so arrogant? I must be dreaming. But, no, this is no nightmare!

And here I sit on the cellar steps, in the terrifying tomb that was once a comforting womb, with only a box of matches to keep the vermin at bay, clutching Peg's dusty picture, my legacy, as I stare in horrified fascination at a wraith of pipe-smoke wafting across the deepening gloom, towards the casement, and into my nostrils and stinging eyes.

ANNIVERSARY

Henry Benjamin is a rotter; he admits it, but only to himself and his best buddy Bertrand at the golf club. Somewhere in the dark recesses of his conscience, Henry prefers to think himself pragmatic or simply hedging his bets. Here he is, raincoat flapping, getting into his huge American car with two enormous bouquets, one for his wife, Wendy, the other for his mistress, Melody.

Well, he can afford it, can't he? As the owner of a thriving business, with homes here and abroad, plus love nest, together with the accoutrements of a successful fifty-year-old man, he should be wallowing in happiness, especially considering his humble beginnings spent in a grimy back-to-back terrace in the shadow of several dark satanic factories, and soaking the dirt off in a tin bath in front of the fire of a Sunday morning. Yes, a man like Henry should have more than a modicum of humility, also bearing in mind his freckles, pale skin and wild red hair.

But is he wallowing? No! What Henry really desires above all else is the fruit of his loins, offspring, children; preferably two boys, thank you very much - an heir and a spare; but one would do very nicely, and even a girl would be acceptable.

Yes, a female child, if properly educated in the ways of wheeling and dealing, might be very good indeed. Henrietta, for that would be her name, may have more insight and/or mental agility than a lad, as no-one knows better than Henry that women are capable of doing more than one thing at a time. He well remembers his own mother reading, listening to the radio, smoking, knitting a fair-isle cardigan, chatting and rocking the pram with one foot, all at the same time. Who could forget that? Such a natural feat of dexterity and co-ordination stays with the admiring observer. A one-man band had nothing on Mummy.

But a boy might be more focused, Henry is deciding. Yes, young Harry would be guided in his father's methods, never straying to right nor left, but ploughing a straight furrow, metaphorically speaking, in the boardroom of GIP Global.

Bertrand is very supportive, and Henry so grateful to his friend for the hint about conserving one's seed, not using it up too often, as that weakens the sperm count, apparently.

Now back to earth and down to the job in hand which is trying to keep his women on an even keel.

First for a bouquet tonight is Melody, Henry's erstwhile secretary who seduced him two years ago, early on in her typing career, fittingly enough behind the filing cabinet. It wasn't that difficult; Henry had been feeling desperate about his lack of success in the progeny department, and needed a boost.

Things moved on quickly from there, as Melody wished with all her heart to be a lady of leisure in order to meet her married girlfriends for lunch and shopping, and this was a quick and easy way of achieving her aim. Still, she works very hard in her chosen niche, managing to retain a certain amount of mystery in order to keep Henry compliant, hand in wallet.

Tonight, she greets him with more than usual warmth, and he sees she is looking very voluptuous this evening, probably because of that expensive negligee she's almost wearing. He notices her pupils are very large indeed. Is she on something? Henry cannot help wondering.

'I can't stay very long, darling. You remember it's the wedding anniversary tonight. I can't keep Wendy waiting too long.'

'Oh, my goodness Henry, I think you'll stay when I tell you what I'm giving you for supper.'

'Not now, Melody, don't act the giddy goat. I can't let Wendy down again, not on our anniversary. You know the score. I can see you tomorrow night – all night.'

'This time, you'll want to let her down – with a bump. Henry – I went to the doctor's today, and, on the subject of bumps, guess what?' Melody's manner is triumphant, her eyes growing wider and darker.

Henry stops in his tracks. 'Darling, you don't mean?' He is stunned into disbelief by the implication of her words, visions of ginger-haired babies dancing before his eyes.

'Yes, Henry, we're pregnant – this time we've hit the jackpot. The baby's due in six months, and I want us to be married before then, all done and dusted.'

'Oh darling,' Henry is so thrilled and overcome thinking of little Harry or, at a push, Henrietta, that he collapses into Melody's arms.

'But I was abroad three months ago,' he suddenly remembers, surfacing and holding her at arms' length.

'Oh don't be silly, Henry, the clinic can only make a rough estimate at this stage.'

'Yes, sorry darling,' and he burrows back into Melody's neck, her fluffy fair hair tickling his nose.

Who's a lucky boy, then? Now he has everything he ever wanted in life, plus a redheaded child to lead his lucrative business into the future.

They sit wrapped around each other for several minutes, lost in thought, until Melody, impatient, breaks the spell, whining, 'Henry darling, you don't love Wendy any more, you said so; she's too old now anyway – probably going through the change already – you said how she's piling on weight. She's definitely missed the boat now I'm expecting. Henry, I want you to tell her tonight about us. This time you must do it. Make a clean break. No backing out. Promise?'

'Yes, I promise; this time I really will tell her. Our married life has been a sham for months. After all, she'll want for nothing when we're divorced. The silly girl, it's not as if she'll be isolated in a high-rise block, living on Social Security.'

Henry is already rehearsing his reasoned argument for later and feels elated at the way things are going, the best outcome for everyone concerned, although he still has a strange feeling of tenderness for flaxen-haired Wendy after twenty years of marriage, even though she has grown quite plump recently.

Naturally, Melody delays Henry far longer than usual tonight, but eventually he manages to escape and drives home in agitated excitement, thinking of the ordeal to come.

'Hello love, are you there?' Henry is puzzled by the lack of a welcoming light as he unlocks the front door into the gloomy hall and, entering with some trepidation, rushes into the darkened Swedish kitchen, to switch on the light.

In a whirl, Henry sees a neatly typed note on the counter-top, which reads:

"*Henry dear,*
I am sorry to dump on you so suddenly, but you know how I've been putting on weight? Well, the reason is that I've been having fertility treatment and finally got pregnant with twins, only they're not yours of course,

as you haven't been near me for over a year. Try to take this calmly, Henry. That temper of yours matches your red hair.

For the past year I've been seeing Bertrand who is like a brother to you, so I hope that will make you feel a bit better – rather like keeping it in the family. We're going to his Tasmanian ranch where we intend to settle. I know you won't miss me too much, and you'll be free to see Melody, if that's what you want. Yes, I've known all along about her – Bertrand told me.

But did you know she started seeing someone else the last time you were abroad? I have to tell you for your own good, as you're so gullible. It's that Italian chap in Sales, Mario somebody. Apparently, rumour has it that Melody likes short, swarthy men. Goodness only knows what she sees in you - you're the complete opposite, simply not her type. Well, I've got a plane to catch, so take care of yourself. And remember, darling, don't smoke in bed.

Love as always, Wendy"

Naturally, Henry is heartbroken. For a brief, mad moment there, he was expecting three babies! He could have coped with that, juggling two families, but now he finds he has no babies, nor, indeed, women.

But just wait until tomorrow – he'd call Melody's bluff in no uncertain terms and, furthermore, give that Mario fellow a good rollicking – must think of a good reason though, as romancing the boss's mistress isn't really a sacking offence, to be fair.

But Henry hasn't got where he is today by being downcast for long, and quickly starts thinking ahead. Hmm, perhaps he should not have condemned fertility treatment out of hand – nothing wrong with a little help.

'And that little Yorkshire lass in Accounts I've had my eye on, what's her name? Oh yes, Molly, erm – something; yes, good solid breeding stock – quite plain, but with the redeeming feature of lovely auburn hair'.

Yes, things will be different from now on; Henry doesn't want any more gorgeous blondes, thanks very much! You simply cannot trust them to be faithful, apparently.

DEATHDAY

I think I must be dying – I heard them talking. Yes, I did. They think I can't hear, but I'm not dead yet, not quite. They can't wait to get rid and divide the spoils, the ratbags. But that's my family for you. Still, it's no more nor less than I deserve, I suppose, but what a shame it's my birthday today – and my deathday too, apparently.

So this must be my deathbed. It's not a very comfortable deathbed, either; a bit too hard for my liking, although I'm not in any pain, per se. This morphine drip is doing a good job here, luckily. We must be grateful for small mercies in situations like this.

And what's that bright light over in the corner. Is it Nurse Robson's torch dazzling my eyes? She's a pretty girl and no mistake. Her first name is Allegra – very nice indeed. No common or garden Joans, Jeans or Pats these days – people have a funny idea that kids will live up to their posh names. There could be a glimmer of truth in that, I suppose. Shame my parents, being of the humble variety, saw fit to call me Herbert – that's probably why I never got very far in life.

Anyway, I've tried to pinch Nurse Robson's bottom once or twice, but she just laughs and skips out of the way, with a smoothly practised movement. Lovely teeth, she has, too.

But I digress…

Could the mysterious spotlight possibly be my guardian angel coming to fetch me? The angel in the corner – I read a book by that name once but can't seem to recall just now what the storyline was. It was written by Monica Dickens, if I'm not mistaken. She was a good writer – took after her great grandfather, what was his name now? I forget.

And I'm wandering again. Come on, Herbert, concentrate. What I need is more time - maybe two years? I promise to be good, honestly I do; oh, all right dammit, two weeks then, or two minutes… That's all I need to…

Hmm, where was I? Must have dropped off for two or three seconds, and now that light seems to be beckoning me to follow, so I guess this is it, folks. Goodbye cruel world, here I go.

Oops, what's happening now? I appear to be climbing up some steps; no, it's a glittery sort of crystal stairway really – could be going up to Heaven, if I'm lucky. I must have died after all, by the looks of things. Shame that, I could have tried to put a few things right before slinging my hook, so to speak.

Anyway, who is this looming up through the puffs of cotton wool in a long kaftan – it's never St Peter, is it? Funny, I thought he'd be a lot taller. But maybe he's not going to let me in – perhaps he'll send me down to the other place. Blast it! I do hope not. Never could stand too much heat, and I don't much relish being dug in the ribs with a trident, or whatever it is they use for jabbing you with. I've always been a temperate creature myself – even cold, according to some people who shall be nameless, which is why I didn't go on those continental holidays very often. But I could have paid for the family to go – oh I wish I could undo some stuff. I was such a skinflint. Now for goodness sake, Herbert, stop this and pull yourself together. Men of my age don't cry – dead people can't cry. And repentant tears can only be second best, whatever way you look at it.

What's he saying, this chap in the white robe and long beard, something about it's not my deathday, and I still have some time to spare. What can it mean?

Maybe he's sending me back; could be I'm recovering from that heart attack.

He appears to be advising me to have another stab at getting into Heaven – apparently you get more than one chance if you've been only slightly wicked, and especially if you kick the bucket on your birthday. Well, it's better than being sent down to the hot place. Alleluia and Amen to that! I wonder what became of Purgatory – you don't hear so much of that nowadays; it's gone out of fashion, most likely.

Oh no, here's another blinding light, only this time it's the sun streaming through a tall window – plus, I have a very strange sensation now, as if I've shrunk or been through a sausage machine. And there's a fellow in a white coat with a steth – stetho – one of those tube things round his neck, saying something to me – well, he's looking in my direction – sounds like, "look at your new-born daughter". How's that again? I wasn't aware of any pregnancy – I thought it was a heart attack, and furthermore I happen to be a chap of the masculine gender, if that helps my case. Maybe I've made medical history. I'll be rich, I tell you, rich!

But let's see if everything is where it should be. Oh yes, I can feel my eyes, nose and mouth are all present and correct - ouch, steady on - poked myself in the eye then; yes, my arms appear a trifle unwieldy – I can't quite reach the old nether regions to carry out a check, but I can move my legs quite a bit. In fact my limbs are waving about most of the time, come to think of it. Why can't I control them? My co-ordination is usually excellent for a man of seventy.

I am speaking to the white coat now, 'Well anyway, doc, thank you for getting me better. When can I go home?' But, strangely, the only sound I hear is a loud wailing. How very odd. I'm normally quite an articulate person. This is all most annoying. And while we're on the subject, why do I feel starving hungry? A nice plate of steak and chips would go down very well, but, failing that, a long drink of milk also appeals. How strange – I don't usually like cowjuice very much…

I'm trying to crane my neck round now, to see if anyone has brought my clothes so I can get dressed and go home. But who is this beautiful young woman with soft curly fair hair looking down at me? I must say she has such an unearthly expression of affection on her face. I shall stop trying to speak and gaze back. She is quite radiant. Is this my guardian angel? She obviously admires me greatly, in spite of the fact that I can't be looking my best at present, feeling as if I've been dragged through a hedge backwards. Have I gone to Heaven after all? Is this some joke played by the Almighty on an unworthy human?

Now, who is this bloke with a black beard peering at me with a funny expression – well, it's more of a stunned one, actually. What's he got to do with this business? He doesn't seem to be a doctor, unless he's off duty in his denims. Old Black Beard's taking pictures of me now. I'm telling him to stop until someone can lend me a mirror; I'm not being vain but I do prefer to look tidy.

But hang on a cotton-picking moment here; suddenly I'm thinking "déjà vu" - this sort of thing has happened to me before.

Oh yes - it all comes back to me now! This is St Peter's way of giving an unworthy sinner another chance of entering the Kingdom of Heaven; a fresh start, going out and coming in again, a clean slate – call it what you will. Just call me the Flying Dutchman, going round and round, maybe forever, until - what? Who knows? It's all a mystery to me, really.

This time, I must really try to remember these things but, of course, my insight will vanish, as usual, long before I can speak although I will do my very best to tell them my secret, every waking hour, as loudly as possible.

But what is more, I'm a girl. That should be a bit more fun! I seem to recall that I've always been a boy previously, although I can't be sure of that now. And I certainly do appreciate being provided with a beautiful doting mother to keep me on the straight and narrow. Will she teach me to cook and clean – you know, all that girlie stuff? I wonder what her name is? She looks to me like a Sarah. Oh, I wonder what she'll call me? I hope it's not Allegra or anything too soppy. Now, Alexandra is nice: that is a name I've always liked – proper upper-class without being too toffee-nosed. I hope that's what they call me.

And, dear Lord, I promise, things will be different – honestly! Thank you God the Father, thank you Baby Jesus, oh and also the Holy Ghost – can't leave him out, although I'm always a touch wary there. Waah, all this thinking is making me so hungry now…..

'Quick, young lady, I mean Mummy, where's my breakfast?'

Oh drat, someone's turned on that wailing noise again.

Alleluia and Amen!

ONE WON'T HURT

'...and Cissie sent me this huge box of crystallised ginger – she knows I'm on a diet, the naughty thing, but I suppose one won't hurt,' announces Aunt Maggie, delicately choosing a large piece with her long painted finger-nails and stuffing it between her cherry-red lips. 'Well, anyway,' she continues through a mouthful of sugary sweetmeat, and already scrabbling for another, 'Cyril says he likes me with a bit of flesh on my bones, aha ha ha.'

Honestly, how pathetic – she's such an embarrassment. Oh, I hate these family parties, so irritating and boring! No cousins here this time – probably got better things to do like going out with their friends and things. How did I get press-ganged into spending New Year's Eve with a load of wrinklies! Oh God, it's still only ten o'clock – another two hours to go before the great escape. I was actually hoping Cousin Craig would turn up and bring that hunky Daniel with him. No such luck! What a shame I'm at an all girls' school.

And on the subject of dieting, just look at this spread, how on earth will I cope? We sat down to a huge dinner only two hours ago, not that I ate much of it – really must try to lose some weight. That's my New Year's resolution. I'll make an early start this very minute and stick to dry crackers and plain water.

But now Aunt Maggie is making her way over with that damned box of crystallised ginger, telling everyone to take a piece as "one won't hurt". Is that her favourite saying? Does she really believe that?

'Come on now, Sophie, help me out.' Bloody Hell, if only she could see herself, turning on the charm, her smile revealing lipstick smears on her teeth.

'No thanks, Auntie – I've had enough to eat for today.'

'Oh, a big strapping girl like you! Large ladies like us can't live on fresh air, you know. We need sustenance! Come on Sophie – one won't hurt.'

Grrr, if I hear her say that one more time, I swear I won't be responsible. 'I love your decorations, Auntie – did you do them yourself?' But she ignores this, has already swanned off and is now torturing some other poor overweight devil.

I'm suddenly aware of someone breathing down my neck and turn instinctively. 'Hello, Sophie! You still here with us oldies? You should be out with your friends. Haven't you got any friends? How are you doing at school – you should be in the big girls' very soon.'

'Oh, Granny, I've been in the big girls', I mean senior school, for four years now. I start O levels next term – I keep telling you.'

'Gah, rubbish – no-one tells your old Granny anything, Sophie. Never do, never did. You should know that! I keep telling you. Have you had any of Aunt Maggie's delicious crystallised ginger? She got it from Cissie. Cissie lives in Spain, you know.'

'Um, yes, I know, but I don't like too many sweets, if you remember.'

'Oh, I hope you're not on one of these new-fangled diets – what a wet blanket, Sophie. Such a miserable kid, always. Your eyes were too near your bladder, in my opinion. You never could stop blubbing. Wailing and weeping, complaining and crying at the slightest thing. Thoroughly spoilt, that's you. I expect it's why you haven't any friends. You only live once, join in the fun.' She pushed a plate of pork pies towards me – 'come on, duckie, one won't hurt – it's not as if you could ever be a model, not with those childbearing hips – you get them from your mother.'

Oh, Heavens above, help me! If only I'd stayed at home with my Christmas books. I don't mind being on my own. Mum and Dad will have to come without me next time. I must say my waistband does feel rather too tight for comfort and I could do with loosening my bra a notch or three. Still, I won't eat anything else tonight, and starting tomorrow I'll go on that new taste-free diet for three months; that's what you have to do in order to get the full benefit, apparently. The less taste, the less you'll eat, that's the principle of it, according to the book of rules they sent me. Urgh, as long as it's not too bloody boring!

Of course, I could always have my jaws clamped, although I've heard it doesn't do the teeth a lot of good. But I would try it if necessary. If I had to choose between that and never seeing Daniel again, I'd choose the jaw-wiring! Eek! It must be love! Now where's my calorie-counter. I'm sure I put it in my handbag. Oh yes, here it is. According to this, I've had 2,300 calories today. But I did have my breakfast standing up at the sink, so that may not count as much. Hmm, let's see - deduct 300 cals, which makes a total of 2,000. Not too bad for New Year's Eve.

Now just look at the buffet table groaning under all that food – it's immoral. Turkey, boiled ham and mince pies, beef, lamb and tongue, mousse and pâté, oh what a nightmare it all is.

I shall just skulk in this corner, holding on to my glass of water for appearance sake. If I stay standing up I'll be burning a few more calories off.

But maybe I'll just move along the table and admire the way Auntie Maggie has presented it all. It is very attractive, actually. Full marks to her. She must have put in a lot of effort. I expect Uncle Cyril and Granny helped her, though.

But just look at this – there's pudding, trifle and ice cream in a cooler, all sorts of sweets, chocolate and pastries, custard and jelly, cashews, brazil nuts, crisps, Cheese Footballs and Twiglets.

Arrgh, sod it! I can't let Auntie Maggie down, see all her hard work go to waste! I'm going to have some of this and forget about my weight. It's more than flesh and blood can stand. I'll start my diet tomorrow. Now, let me at it, pile it on, pile it on, savoury and dessert can go on the same plate – yum, yum. Just one of each thing won't hurt.

'Oh Sophie, surely you're not going to eat all that?' Granny is cackling from somewhere across the room. 'Look everyone, the girl has eyes bigger than her belly.'

Ashamed, I gaze red-faced round the crowded room through a mist; then a familiar voice at my shoulder breaks into my misery.

'Hey, Sophie,' Daniel is saying, 'Pucker up, I've got a belated Christmas present for you – a sprig of mistletoe; how about a New Year's kiss? Don't be shy, just one won't hurt.'

I put down the heaped plate and turn my smiling face up to Daniel's; how fantastically fabulous – somehow I seem to have lost my appetite!

HOME FROM HOME

So here we are again, already halfway through another season and I have a No Vacancies sign up in the front window as per. I've never had any trouble letting the rooms and, even though I says it as shouldn't, we are very, very select here at Albatross House – some people come back time after time.

Take for instance Mr and Mrs Gresham, an elderly couple I've known since the year dot, and whose idea of holiday heaven is to sit in one of those shelters on the promenade, come rain or come shine, on account of Mrs Gresham being a martyr to prickly heat. She favours twin-set and pearls, and he sports a yellow paisley cravat, so I know they are respectable citizens although I don't know much else about them except they hail from Wolverhampton.

They are rather particular about food though, which is a nuisance, and, apart from the usual charge of sixpence per week for the cruet, I charge them an extra two shilling per week for supplying fresh-baked granary bread (which they like toasted just so) and genuine Scotch marmalade.

I always get my Wilf to serve breakfast as I am *not* a morning person and Michelle doesn't come in until eleven to help Mrs Montgomery with the lunches. Michelle's a French student over for the summer. We do have communication problems and I have to shout at the top of my voice to get her to understand. It's all tiresome, I know, but she accepts a low wage, so "san fairy-ann" as they say in her country of birth.

I insist that *all* tips are put into a special lidded pot which I empty each day, and accumulated gratuities are distributed at the end of the season – but if any staff member leaves before that, they do *not* share.

I'm a *people* person, me – I love the human race, yes, even foreigners like the French girl – makes no odds, although I once had a student from Wales applying for a job and I had to turn her down; not because I'm prejudiced or anything, oh no, certainly not – it was on behalf of my residents who may object to hymns being sung at them through the serving hatch. I've heard about the Welsh and they are all strict chapel – Baptist, I think it is – well-known for their singing.

Tch, there's a Mr and Mrs Stoneycroft staying in the second floor front this week. She's only a slip of a thing, can't be more than twenty, but they already have a little kiddie, a girl of about two, and it looks as if another one's on the way. I almost turned down their booking as I really can't risk my residents, or myself, being kept *awake* at night by crying kiddies but, luckily, this one's kept quiet so far. Huh, they actually asked me to baby-sit while they went to the pictures but I said I'd let them know later on which gave me time to come up with an excuse. It was a bit cheeky of them really because this is my home too and I need my rest and relaxation after working so hard all day long. Anyway, I instructed my Wilf to tell them we had friends coming over every evening this week. After all, if we ran a babysitting service it'd say so in the advert.

Mind you, I wasn't best pleased when the two young women in the first floor front offered to look after the toddler as a favour. Well, that's girls for you, they love playing with babies, it doesn't matter whose.

But it tickles me how lasses all look the same these days with their waspie waists, full skirts and flatties, ooh and what with their comical black-rimmed eyes and long blonde hair flapping, hoping it'll attract the lads. I got my Wilf to warn them that followers are not allowed in this guest house because I've *heard* about these two females out on the prowl, walking on the prom in their 30 denier nylons that they rinse out every night in the washbasin in spite of a notice pinned to the wall requesting patrons *not* to drape wet items of clothing about the bedrooms. I told my Wilf to mention it to them but he said it wasn't his place to discuss items of intimate apparel with young ladies of the opposite sex.

Oh, he's hopeless at times, too polite by far, so I turned my snarl into a tight little smile and stood, feet apart, arms folded, waiting for them as they came, giggling and pushing, through the front door.

'Oops, hello, Mrs Stebbings,' they spluttered, bouncing up the stairs like startled rabbits. *They* knew what they'd done all right, and I hadn't even opened my mouth. By the way, I really must get my Wilf to replace that light bulb in the hallway, it's so dark you can hardly see for looking, *and* he should speak to Mrs Montgomery about the horrible smell of cabbage hanging about – it gets in up your nose something shocking. Because, if the stupid woman didn't boil the greens for *such* a long time, the *atmosphere* would be improved no end.

Tch, there's a courting couple here this week, asked for a double room, they did; so I got my Wilf to read them the riot act, by which I mean the house rules, and consequently we now have the man in the third floor back, and the female in the first floor front – as far apart as possible. *I'm* not being party to any goings on, oh no, not in my establishment – over my dead body. They can do what they *like* at home but on these premises they will follow the Albatross House policy, which is: No sex, please – this is *Yorkshire*!

Now, I am *not* an afternoon person and I was having a bit of a rest after lunch the other day, feet up,

Terry's All Gold in easy reach, looking over Wilf's accounts, when I must have closed my eyes for, well, only a second or two. I was disturbed by a loud rapping on the door of my sitting-room (or the penthouse, as I call it if I happen to be feeling waggish which, I admit, isn't very often) and who should shuffle through, red in the face, but Elsie the cleaner, Ada the chambermaid and Lillian the general dogsbody.

'Coo, look what the cat's dragged in,' I said. 'To what do I owe the pleasure.'

'Can we have a word with you, Mrs Stebbings,' they said.

'What about?' I said, 'can't you see I'm busy?'

'Well, we was wanting to, er, to ask for a pay rise,' they said.

'*Was* you – *was* you, indeed?' I said, 'I think you'd better talk to Mr Stebbings about that.'

'Oh, we 'ave,' they said, 'and Wilf said to teck it up wi' you.'

'Oh, he *did, did* he?' I said, 'I'll knock his block off! But in any case, it's *Mr Stebbings* to you, and, as Mr Stebbings should have stated, the answer is No, because you'll never get another job anywhere else mid-season so I'm doing you a favour keeping you on when I should sack the lot of you for gross insubordination and for being so cheeky – now, move it!'

'Oh, right-ho, Mrs Stebbings,' they said, bowing and scraping, backing out of the doorway. You see? Problem solved! I have to keep a firm hand on deck, otherwise these people will walk all over the place.

Of course, I tore into Wilf later on when he came in after supervising dinner. 'Why do you let the staff call you Wilf?' I said, 'you'll *never* get respect if you're too cosy with 'em.'

'Nay, Gladys, love,' he said, 'what's to do? I'm only being pleasant and it's better to have a nice friendly house.'

'Friendly house?' I said. 'By heck, it's a damned sight more than just a friendly house. Why do you think Mr and Mrs Gresham come back year after year? Ask 'em; you know what they'll say! They'll say, "Albatross House, it's a home from home". Yes, that's what they'll seh – an 'ome from 'ome. Now, pass me that bag of acid drops, will you – I must have something tart after all that chocolate – ooh, right upset me belly, it has – and it's all *your* doing, you daft begger – get me a smaller box next time! And then you can teck these accounts over – me eyes are too tired to do any more – oh, and put t'telly on, it's nearly time for that Cliff Richards.'

Well – after watching Cliff and his lads (*I forget what they're called just at the minute, but ooh, I love that Hank Martin in his horn-rimmed specs*) – erm, where was I, oh yes, after watching that Cliff Richards and his Wotsnames singing "Move It", I took meself off to bed 'cos I was right worn out and, anyway – tell the truth – I've *never* been much of an *evening* person, really.

Some People

PRETTY SURE

I can get on with anybody, I'm pretty sure of that. I always have the other person's interests at heart, can see both sides of an argument and from an early age felt it was my role in life to look after others. Kindness itself, my mother used to say – "Audrey is kindness itself".

It wasn't just that though, it was my duty too. You know how it can go, an only child born to middle-aged parents never flies the nest, which is how I came to be rattling around in this large detached house full of dark paintwork, big brown wardrobes and chests of drawers full of darned socks, lisle stockings, corsets and candlewick housecoats.

And once I came to realise both my parents had gone for good, I felt desolate, at a loss, in a vacuum, and I couldn't face the immense task of sorting out, although I did gather up and throw away all those mothballs my mother was so fond of scattering about the bedrooms: the smell of camphor, however, lingers still.

I had continued to go to work during my mother's final illness, which was mercifully short, and so I had plenty of human contact at the office on a daily basis. I always felt ready to dispense advice from my fount of knowledge and was invariably willing to lend a few pounds to some less thrifty soul before payday.

My colleagues were very tactful after my bereavement and thoughtfully left me alone to get on with my work. I was not pressed for gory details, neither was I asked about the funeral, and my workmates even went as far as assuming I wouldn't want to attend the Christmas party, which I did appreciate immensely as I'm afraid these social occasions are too boisterous for me; and, apart from the rawness of my recent loss, I am a lifelong teetotaller.

It was in the New Year when Katrina, my opposite number in Marketing, asked if I would meet her after work.

She went on to say that if I didn't mind she'd like to "pick my brains" – a term I find singularly repulsive.

However, as I said, I am very interested in other people's problems and also I was wondering whether it might present a good opportunity to mention the money I had lent her last October or should I just let it pass.

I felt certain she had simply forgotten about it – yes, I was pretty sure of that. Katrina is some years younger than me, but we have always worked well together – in fact, I may have mentioned that I can get on with anybody.

She had a sad tale to tell in the café that evening – her life was in disarray; she had caught her partner having an affair and was ready to leave him for good, her bags packed and everything. She had nowhere to go and wanted my help in her search for alternative accommodation.

I was more than eager to assist; in fact, I was quite excited by the prospect and it would be something of a diversion for me in my present fog of bereavement.

The next day being a Saturday, we trawled around the accommodation agencies together and rang newspaper advertisements from my home telephone, all to no avail. The suitable properties had already been snapped up, or were too expensive or were not yet ready for occupation.

Katrina wept bitterly and said she could not bear to spend one more night under the same roof as that two-timing beast.

An idea struck me, and I hesitated, but only for a split second.

As I may have mentioned, I can get on with anybody, and my proposed solution, albeit of a temporary nature, would be of benefit to both of us. Katrina made a play of declining – oh no, I couldn't put you to all that trouble – but in the end I escorted the poor girl round to her flat.

We picked up her bags and other possessions which were blocking the hallway – many more items than I had anticipated, if I'm being truthful, which necessitated three trips in my car, and then the following day I hired a van to transport the larger items of furniture.

'This is only until I find a place of my own,' Katrina is fond of saying when she gets in my way or I have occasion to make a mild complaint about her cigarette ash which she flicks everywhere. 'Oh, fetch me a saucer then, if you're so particular – any civilised person would provide ashtrays'.

Quite truthfully, she's a scream – I throw my head back and roar at her little jokes – because they are jokes, yes, I'm pretty sure of that. Katrina has a wicked sense of humour and she *is* very bright, although domestic science as a subject seems to be a closed book to her.

I pride myself on being a tolerant person and raised no objections when she proposed shifting some of my heavy furniture from her room and replacing it with her more modern stuff – 'this is only temporary, Audrey, and we can stash yours in the basement for safekeeping'.

A friendly chap called Jason came round to help us, and he seemed very capable.

Jason also offered to decorate my bedroom for me, 'let some light in, get rid of this dark brown and institutional green, eh, Audrey?'

He made helpful suggestions too, like, why didn't I take the small third bedroom in order to escape the fumes while he was stripping the paint, which showed he had a real interest in my well-being and not only in the hourly rate I was paying him. I was touched by his concern and forethought, and so I went along with his sensible ideas. 'It *is* only temporary, Audrey,' Katrina assured me for the umpteenth time as they moved my narrow bed to the box-room.

Katrina invited Jason to stay for tea, and I must say I got on swimmingly with him – such an amusing sense of the ridiculous: he showed us the dragon tattoo on his back, but I was even more fascinated watching the sunlight glinting on his nose stud and eyebrow ring when he laughed, which was often. As I may have mentioned, I can get on with anybody.

We giggled all through the cheese on toast and, after that, Jason was a regular visitor, getting on with the decorating each evening and sometimes staying overnight. At first I was horrified by the nocturnal noises coming from the other side of the wall but at the same time felt mighty relieved I had kept myself to myself all these years, never dipping my toe, so to speak, into such goings-on; it all sounded surprisingly violent, not that I'd ever given that sort of thing a lot of thought. Perhaps it was normal? I bought some earplugs.

A couple of months after this, I went to the doctor as I began to feel quite poorly, and angina was diagnosed. I was strongly advised to avoid all stress so took the decision to take early retirement on health grounds and was awarded a full pension.

I hinted mildly to Katrina that I might prefer to manage alone now that I was retired, but she was outraged and went on about how could she desert me at a time like this, how could she leave me alone in my hour of need, even though she and Jason had that *very* morning seen a suitable flat to rent, but, no, she would put my interests first and stay put, it was the least she could do, and anyway Jason hadn't finished decorating my bedroom yet! I had neither energy nor courage to argue and let it pass. I realise they are both very good to me and I'd hate for Katrina to think I was ungrateful.

And now I've just been rudely awoken from my Sunday afternoon nap by deafening music from downstairs; midwinter gloom has crept through my tiny window and the electric-light switch is loose and doesn't seem to be working.

Fortunately, I do pride myself on being an efficient and practical person and have therefore kept a candle and a box of matches in each room of the house ever since we had those power cuts a few years ago.

But, *oh dear*! Now my bedroom door appears to be jammed; it won't budge, and they can't hear me shouting over the din – honestly, that Jason, he's such a joker – leads Katrina astray, he does.

I'm pretty sure they'll be devastated when I tell them how frightened I've been, trapped in here in the dark, with this flickering candlelight throwing grotesque shapes on the walls, because I know they'll stop this larking around soon and let me out for my tea. Mm, I'm looking forward to my tea – I think we're having cheese on toast again this evening – yes, I'm pretty sure of that.

OTHER PEOPLE

I've been watching Diana Catchpole painting her front gate a horrible shade of vermillion, which is the only description for such a vile colour. Vile Vermillion it should say on the paint-tin. I'm sure she knows I'm watching her through the spy-hole in my front door from the way she stops to chat to any passer-by, nodding and smiling in that irritating way of hers, obviously trying to demonstrate her popularity; yet she never has a smile for me – more of a rictus, I'd say.

Of course, all this is part of her plan to annoy me, in revenge for my dogs getting into her back garden and leaving their little calling cards on her manicured lawns. Stupid woman – so proud of her silly garden – she has the wrong set of priorities in life. I mean to say, animals are more important than grass, flowers and shrubs. In fact, what harm can my little doggies do?

And when she erected wire fencing out of spite, I cut a hole at the bottom so that my little darlings could get through again. I replied "love me love my dogs" through the letterbox when she came round rapping on the knocker. I was actually too upset to open the door to her. Oh, I can't abide people who don't love animals, and also I find the woman quite frightening, always moaning on about something.

Anyway, after she'd mended the hole I felt like planting a couple of leylandii against the fence as some sort of self-assertive statement, and this has now grown almost eight feet high, leaning towards her conservatory, blocking out the sunlight to some extent, I admit – but just let me catch her touching it with a pair of shears and I'll be straight round the council offices. I know my rights, I know the law.

Mrs Catchpole seems to disapprove of everything I do. She actually yelped when she saw me riding my bicycle on the pavement. Honestly, some people – as if I'm going to risk life and limb cycling on the road, and, please, I only went over her toe the tiniest bit! Just let her bring the authorities into this and I'll tell them the facts: even the postmen ride on the footpath, so I'm not the only one by any means, and she always has a kind word and a nod for them. Why am I so different?

Then there's my six beautiful cats. She can't stop them getting onto her property, try as she might. I mean to say, it's not my fault the catnip ended up on her side of the fence and now, of course, every moggie in the neighbourhood makes a beeline for her garden. Poetic justice, I call it!

I like to use my barbecue on suitably warm days, but Mrs Diana Catchpole doesn't like the smell of sausages and steak, apparently. She pushed a note through my door, saying she's a vegetarian and why do I have to cook meat outside especially when her washing is on the line. Honestly, the nerve of the woman! I ignored the note as I can do what I like on my own property and no-one else has complained.

To tell the truth, I do actually wait until the wind is blowing her way only because her house is on the end of this row and I wouldn't want the rest of the neighbours being troubled by my smoke – I couldn't tell her that though, I don't want to give her any ammunition against me. But you can see that I am a very sensitive and considerate person.

Next news, just because I was burning my garden rubbish and some pieces of old furniture on a nice big bonfire, she very pointedly took her washing off the line. I've never known anyone do so much

Some People

laundry! She lives on her own and must change the bed-linen every other day judging by all the sheets she pegs out. I like the smell of a garden bonfire, I must say. Mrs Catchpole doesn't appear to like anything!

Anyway, later that day, whilst enjoying a musical interlude, I was really upset when she rapped loudly on the party wall between our two properties and then ten minutes later on my front door. 'I've been knocking on your wall for the past hour,' she said, her cheeks two spots of bright red. 'Oh, is that right?' I replied, 'I couldn't hear you for the music. How can I help you?'

'Mrs Stradling,' she said, 'it's the music I came about – could you please turn it down, for pity's sake – not everyone likes Wagner, and I can hardly hear myself thinking – these party walls are only one brick thick, you know.'

'Mrs Catchpole,' I replied, suddenly feeling brave, 'you are frightening me – please stop knocking on my wall and my door and sending me notes accusing me of this and that, otherwise I shall have to report you to the authorities. I don't interfere with your life, I've never made the slightest complaint against you, so kindly leave me alone.'

In my own defence, it's worth mentioning here that I only play Wagner between the hours of 8 a.m. and 11 p.m., never during the night, and in that way I keep within the rules. I know my rights, I know the law.

The next day she pushes a note through the letterbox moaning on about my dogs barking during the early hours and how she needs her sleep as she has to get up at the crack of dawn to catch the early bus for work. The silly woman; I'm well aware she only works mornings. If she's that tired she can have a nap in the afternoon, can't she? Some people need their lives organising for them.

Anyway, this time I did write back explaining that my Jack Russells are very well behaved and they only bark if they hear anything unusual and that she should be grateful for having the protection of guard dogs to scare away possible intruders. Naturally, she didn't come back to me on that one!

I mean to say, you will have noted that I am very polite and calm at all times even in face of temper tantrums on my doorstep and impolite notes shoved through the door.

At any event, after receiving one or two letters from the Council which I threw in the bin, I received one from the Arbitration Authority asking me to attend a meeting. I just ignored it. I know my rights and they cannot force me to go. I don't wish to sit opposite Mrs Catchpole having to listen to her catalogue of imaginary gripes. After all, I don't want to sink to her level, bandying arguments and trading insults.

And now I'm considering reporting her to the police for harassment, which is what it boils down to, at the end of the day.

I've kept a diary of her moans and groans, filed all her notes neatly in a folder.

I mean, she's complained about my dogs, my cats, my bicycle, my trees, my barbecue, my bonfire and my music, so much so that I feel like a prisoner in my own house, scared to do anything in case she's monitoring my movements and starts complaining again. I almost think twice before breathing in case Mrs Catchpole might disapprove and report me for using up too much air. She needs her head examining, the woman is as mad as a hatter and she'll make me crazy too if things carry on like this!

Anyway, while I'm thinking what plan of action to take about the situation, I've decided to relax a little, do the same as the madwoman next door and indulge myself with some DIY – after all, this is my house and I should be able to do as I like – now, where did I put my Black & Decker?

PART OF THE FURNITURE

Miss Fanshaw, you could safely say, was no oil-painting! She was scrawny, with feet like barges and a Roman nose. Livid purple smudges under bright beady eyes completed the picture. She reminded me of some huge bird of prey pecking away at her Remington Rand, day after day, in the dusty first floor offices of The Box-Oxford Boot Company. It was said that Miss Fanshaw had never gone home to her bed-sit in Paddington before seven o'clock of an evening nor had she ever taken a holiday and, having perched at that same desk since the year dot, she had become part of the furniture.

Mr Goatley depended upon Miss Fanshaw, knowing without realising it that she would sort out any mess, solve any problems that might arise. 'Look here,' he would bark, throwing a sheaf of invoices onto her tidy desk, 'check Miss Bessermay's calculations – they're miles out.' He barely noticed the creature's grateful flash of prominent teeth in acknowledgment of his oblique compliment. 'Of course, sir,' she'd reply without interrupting the rhythmic movement of her fingers flying over the keys followed by their smooth transition to the adding machine – *tap, tap, tap, brrrrr*!

Mr Goatley liked his frothy coffee served twice a day, together with three fig rolls or, alternatively, two custard creams, fresh supplies of which were kept in a highly-polished brass biscuit tin on Miss Fanshaw's desk. She checked his preferences each morning when taking in the newly-sorted and date-stamped post, ensuring that Mr Goatley's requirements were carried out efficiently, by dint of doing everything herself. No-one else was allowed to interfere in the daily rituals, least of all Phoebe Bessermay who could not seem to get anything right. As for Miss Fanshaw's own refreshment, a cup of hot water with lemon sufficed. She was never seen to eat anything.

One particular evening I was late finishing my filing and it was gone half past six when I left the office, my head aching with stress and fatigue. A nearby pharmacy was my first port of call where I queued for ten minutes in order to purchase aspirin.

When I emerged and turned the corner, I spied Mr Goatley hurrying along the pavement ahead, chatting animatedly to someone, a woman wearing a red cloche hat, but, who it was, I could not discern as he had his arm around her shoulders most protectively.

Intrigued, I quickened my pace, following Mr Goatley and his mysterious companion at a safe distance before they entered a seedy private hotel in one of those shabby thoroughfares leading from Gray's Inn Road, a very disreputable area in those days if you preferred comfort, cleanliness and quiet.

Slowing my pace, I sidled by the glass doors of the hotel, and glimpsed my quarry standing by the reception desk. I suddenly felt guilty and realised I'd been stalking them. I made a quick exit from the scene, fair galloping towards Russell Square tube station in my haste.

The next morning, I looked at Mr Goatley through different eyes! I knew he was married: Mrs Goatley often rang him at the office and he usually ended up shouting angrily at her down the telephone. Maybe she was deaf or perhaps they didn't get on, who knows? However, I realised that his companion of the night before was not his wife because of the tender and solicitous body language displayed. One can sense these things!

Later that same day, Mr Goatley announced that our Managing Director, Mr Box-Oxford, would be making his official visit from Head Office in Mayfair to our little outpost in Bloomsbury at the end of the week. A flurry of activity and tidying up followed, causing such a dust storm to rise that the office looked no better than before. Of course, Miss Fanshaw's little cubby-hole was always kept in a spick and span condition, and so she just carried on with her work, blithely disregarding the rest of us rushing around in a panic.

Mr Box-Oxford's official visits were anticipated with mixed feelings! Not all of us would be awarded praise, a pay-rise or bonus. One or two could be hopeful of their chances if important customers had settled their accounts promptly. Miss Fanshaw could rest assured because she was, of course, the backbone of the office and part of the furniture.

The day dawned and our Managing Director arrived in his Rolls Royce driven by a sullen chauffeur who was made to wait outside in the event a passing ruffian took it into his head to kick the tyres. Eventually, Mr Box-Oxford could be heard climbing the steep wooden staircase, puffing and panting, before finally staggering through the half-glazed double doors, wheezing and red in the face, demanding a drink with which to take his pills.

Mr Goatley was all fluttering attention, but, like magic, Miss Fanshaw appeared, proffering a tray bearing a glass of water, which she had organised as soon as she'd heard Mr Box-Oxford bellowing at his chauffeur in the street below.

When he had stopped choking and spluttering, Mr Box-Oxford stood to attention ready to address the small band of assembled employees.

Apart from Mr Goatley and Miss Fanshaw, there were five accounts clerks and myself. I was the lowly filing clerk and held no hope for my prospects as there are only limited ways one can get files out and put them away again. I knew Phoebe Bessermay was a non-starter as she was still on probation and her work was not up to scratch – even she freely admitted as much one lunchtime in the ladies' toilet as I watched her applying purple shadow to her heavy eyelids. 'I can't add up for toffee,' she'd sniggered, before adding with a rasping cough, 'God, I'm dying for a gasper – got a spare cig on you?'

And now, as our Managing Director commenced his speech, Miss Bessermay perched on a desk swinging one leg, whilst Miss Fanshaw, meek yet confident, stared at the bare floorboards, simpering.

'Ladies and gents,' began Mr Box-Oxford, 'I am sorry to say we have had a bad year, and when I say bad, don't run away with the idea we haven't been shifting boots and shoes, dear me, no; what I mean to say is that we must, we really must get more of our retail customers to pay up on time. These late payers are the very devil for any wholesaler.

'*However* – there is always a silver lining in any cloud and I am pleased to say that even though pay-rises and bonuses have perforce been withheld this time, Mr Goatley has ***strongly*** recommended that Miss Bessermay be taken on to the permanent staff and awarded a small honorarium for trying *so* hard and, of course, she has a degree in mathematics which no-one else in this company, nay, not even myself, can claim.

'I am sure you will all agree that the future of this country is in the hands of – the youth of today and we must give every encouragement to the, to the – youth of – hum, *today*. I thank you for listening –

you're all doing your best – and now I must be off – good day to you.' And he was out of the half-glazed double doors and down that creaking wooden casement like a ferret down a rabbit hole, bad heart or no.

I looked across at Miss Fanshaw who was flashing her teeth in a ghastly grimace of some deep emotion. Everyone else shuffled despondently back to their desks, except for Phoebe Bessermay who pulled out a red cloche hat, rammed it on her head, and made for the half-glazed double doors, announcing with a girlish giggle that she was taking the rest of the day off to impart to her mother the good news. Mr Goatley stood rooted to the bare floorboards, his mouth opening and closing like a fish in what I understood to be disappointment at Miss Bessermay's lack of gratitude.

Some minutes later I began to feel light-headed and went to get a sip of water from the tiny kitchenette on the landing. Miss Fanshaw was already in there busily preparing Mr Goatley's afternoon refreshment. On his personal tray stood a small plate of fig rolls together with the usual coffee mug displaying the initials "PCG" which, as we all knew, indicated Percival Claude Goatley. I stood there like a ghost in the gloom, just beyond the threshold, and saw with my own eyes Miss Fanshaw bending over the mug of coffee, and spit, spit, spitting into it – augmenting the froth, one might say.

Taking a backward step, I turned and silently trod the length of the dark landing before reaching the safety of the office and my green filing cabinet. I cogitated about sharing with her my experience in the street earlier that week but thought better of it – for it is simply not wise to add fuel to the flame of female fury, and, after all, Miss Fanshaw was already taking her revenge, of sorts.

RATS!

A deathly hush fell on the room as I entered. Several pairs of lash-fringed eyes focused on me. Had I lipstick on my teeth? Was my skirt caught up in my knickers?

'Here I am, ladies, ready for my close-up.' I swept a look around the dozen smartly-dressed members of the "Misandrist Club".

The company raised their eyebrows and smiled wryly. Nadine, a scarlet-lipped property developer indicated a bentwood chair, and I sat.

'Felicity, welcome,' Nadine began. 'You'll be aware that Misandrist is Greek for man-hater; the Club stipulates that you must be divorced, be committed to hating men and have no kids.'

'Oh, I avoided that trap – children are a life sentence,' I said. 'And I *am* divorced, my sole purpose now being to making men miserable.'

'Yes, I like that very much,' drawled Greta, a neurotic solicitor with long shapely legs. 'The Club's slogan states "I think, therefore I am single". Are you *sympatico* with that?"

'Definitely,' I replied fiercely. 'In my experience, before marriage a man will lay down his life for you, but after marriage, he won't even lay down his newspaper.'

'Yes, you're right there,' whined Grizelda, a skinny entrepreneur, 'and when a man brings his wife flowers for no reason, there's a reason!'

'Exactly! And as you see, Felicity, we are bitter, but also content,' explained Nadine. 'We've been through the mill – most of us have been married more than once, all to profoundly superficial men, and we agree that the happiest time of life is after your first divorce. One can never recapture that rapture.'

'Yes, quite,' I murmured.

'And personally,' she continued, 'I was married to a Marxist and then a Tory and neither one would take the rubbish out. Plus, I have yet to hear a man ask for advice on how to combine marriage and a career.'

'Ah, but it's better to have loved and lost,' I replied. 'For instance, my sister has never actually *been* married, although she always says she's divorced so people won't think there's something wrong with her.'

'Well, I understand her logic,' fluted Nadine. 'I married beneath me – most women do.'

The others chortled, and Arabella, an emaciated banker, added, 'I wanted a man who was kind and understanding. Is that too much to ask of a millionaire?'

'Well put,' crooned Nadine, 'but we want to know more about Felicity. Are you upwardly mobile, professionally, or are you simply well-bred?'

'If you have to tell people you're a lady – you aren't,' I stated coolly.

'Good answer,' my inquisitor trilled, 'and, just for the hell of it, I would like to state that the problem with joining the rat race is that, even if you win it, you're still a rat! Of course, that refers mainly to men!'

We broke into sophisticated laughter and applause, only interrupted by a young Italian waiter bringing in a tray of coffee.

A deathly hush fell on the room. Then, as one, the assembly moved forward, surrounding him, simpering, fluttering their false eyelashes, stroking the boy's muscular arms until he raised his hands in mock defence.

'Laydees, laydees,' he smiled, showing perfect white teeth. 'Pleeza to sit down-a – I serve you each in turn-a, pleeza, I beg-a you!'

Oh rats! So much for commitment to the cause, I thought, closing the door quietly behind me.

On the way home, I remembered to stop off at Asda to get sweets for the kids and fags for me old man – yes, and something for tea. Ho hum, a woman's work is never done!

SNOWBLIND

Suddenly, lowering storm clouds were blown away in the dying gasps of the blizzard, a frost moon flooded the mountainside with light and a myriad stars appeared, spilling their sugar across the bowl of the sky.

And there I stood, wrapped in a snowdust-sparkling fur coat, my breath hanging crystalline in the freezing air. My heart leapt when I saw the log cabin: I thrilled to the gusts of grey smoke curling from its sturdy chimney, to the glowing windows beckoning with their seductive promise of comfort. I approached and knocked on the heavy wooden door.

And here he was, the man of my dreams framed in the doorway; moonbeams caressed his youthful features, his beautiful face registering shock at the sight of my waiflike figure poised beyond the threshold. Without hesitation he ushered me inside and set me down before a pot-bellied stove. Questions poured from his lips but I merely shrugged, smiled and rubbed my hands before the rosy glow.

The youth brought me food and drink but I refused to tell him my name or how I came to be there, miles from the nearest hamlet. 'In that case, I shall call you Bianca, for the whiteness of the snow,' he said, adding that his name was Sebastian and he had taken the isolated cabin for the winter hoping to finish his thesis. He hesitated for a moment before his natural curiosity got the better of him, and the torrent of questions began afresh, but I shook my head, begging to be allowed to sleep.

Obviously mystified by the strange turn of events, he nonetheless nodded in sympathy at my apparent fatigue. 'Of course you must rest,' he said, quickly making up a truckle bed against the wall and providing me with a pair of fleecy pyjamas that swamped my delicate but shapely frame.

I was aware that he stayed awake, watching me through the long night-time hours but I wanted to bide my time, tease him, play hard to get, draw out the anticipation leading to his, our, inevitable reward, and I knew in my bones there was another blizzard due before dawn.

I awoke next morning to the knowledge we were snowbound and, perforce, would be in each other's company for the duration. That is when we relaxed and grew to know each other, Sebastian and I. Over the following hours, days, weeks, we played games, cooked exotic meals, toasted each other in mulled wine, did jigsaws, danced to romantic music on the wireless and, very soon, he had fallen in love with me. And I – I had loved him since the dawn of time.

'Who are you?' he asked for the hundredth time, and I answered, coquettishly, 'I am a snow sprite, spirit of the frozen mountain; my bounden duty is to drive men wild.'

'Well, you certainly have that effect on this man, at least,' he laughed, drawing me to him and kissing me full on the lips. I felt the warmth of his body against mine, and oh, he was so sweet, this boy, as yet unspoilt by life, untouched by tragedy, unsullied by evil, and here he was, nestling in my arms, and he belonged to me alone.

'I don't want this to end,' he said, stroking my long black hair tenderly, 'I've never seen such sapphire blue eyes, such beauty and grace, that silken skin – you are perfect, perfect: Bianca, the woman without a flaw, plus, you laugh at my jokes – what more could any man ask?' And removing the gold signet ring from his middle finger, he placed it on my thumb. 'Now, we are married,' he pronounced, 'Bianca, my darling, my wife.'

Yes, he adored me, he loved me, really loved me.

How long did our charmed existence continue? I know not; I knew only that we lived in a cocoon of bliss, on a cloud of euphoria, each day more wonderful than the last, and oh, the nights, the nights when our bodies entwined in rapture, so romantic, and yet erotic – yes, erotic. And yet, at the same time, my overwhelming joy was tinged with a certain uneasiness, a tugging at the heart, and I knew that such bittersweet happiness had to end sooner or later, and so did he.

When the snow began to thaw, eaves and trees dripping water, we were holding back each new tomorrow, denying all signs of the end of winter, only our eyes betraying fear of what was to come.

Then the dreaded day dawned. There was a loud knocking, sounds of voices outside the cabin, and the door flew open. *They* came in, their strong hands grasping at my arms, forcing me into my moth-eaten old duffel coat, saying strange things, words that made no sense. In my incomprehension and blind panic, I turned to Sebastian for help but he had gone, vanished into the shadows. 'How can he leave me now, when I need him the most,' I wept. 'Sebastian, oh Sebastian, my sweet love, where are you?'

Distraught, I caught sight of my reflection in an old fly-blown mirror propped against some sticks of broken furniture and was shocked to see my hair was now snow-white, my body gone to a shapeless mass, my paper-thin skin yellow and wrinkled with age, and those sapphire-blue eyes faded and confused.

And then... and then…

…I remembered…

'Come on, Phyllis,' they were urging, not unkindly, 'you shouldn't sit in this gloomy old shed all on your own. Join in with the others, have some fun. We're planning a game of Snakes and Ladders in a moment. That will be jolly, won't it? Now come along, dear, don't struggle, be a good girl; that's right, let's get you back inside, it's time for your tablets.'

I slipped a hand into my duffel coat pocket, and my fingers, stiff with arthritis, closed around the signet ring on my thumb.

ECHO

I recall vividly my first sight of Primrose at a friend's party. The other guests faded into nothingness as I beheld her cloud of ash blonde hair and alabaster skin across a crowded room. Our eyes met, and when at last our fingers touched, I knew her character was as angelic as her appearance. From that moment we were inseparable and no-one was surprised when we married within a few short weeks.

Our honeymoon was spent in a whitewashed Cornish cottage, but we managed to stay only two nights because Primrose, shaking with apprehension, said she could hear rustling in the wainscot and a screaming in the chimney. I said it was most likely mice and seagulls and, in any case, I was there to protect her, but she insisted the place had bad vibes, someone had been murdered there, and she would not be placated. However, I was quite eager to get home to our love nest, which was a small flat at the top of a large Victorian house, and so we hurriedly packed up and left.

Married life was idyllic: we spent every spare moment together, preferring to stay at home and play housekeeping after the day's work.

I was a clerk in the City, and travelled to the office by tube; Primrose worked locally in a school, and thus was able to get home in time to prepare the dinner, put on something more feminine, refresh her lipstick, and have my cardigan and slippers ready for when I came through the front door at about six o'clock.

I couldn't believe my luck in finding Primrose; she was everything a man could desire in a woman: acquiescent, demure, affectionate, passionate, and tireless in carrying out her housewifely duties.

However, there was one small fly spoiling the ointment of our bliss: Primrose was not happy living at the top of the house; she sensed a malign presence in the attics above our heads, particularly during the hour or so before I got home. Once again I explained it was probably mice or perhaps pigeons. Any faint sounds hardly registered with me but I could see that Primrose was troubled. I reported the noises to Mr Rothman, the landlord, and eventually he came along to investigate.

I insisted upon accompanying Mr Rothman aloft, and together we carried out a thorough survey of the attics, inspecting every dark corner with the aid of torches, but all we saw were festoons of dusty cobwebs, like so many lace curtains, studded with huge spiders, but nothing to explain the sounds that unsettled Primrose so much.

I lied and told her we'd found evidence of pigeons, but she was no fool and the next day quickly ascertained from Mr Rothman the true state of affairs.

'There's no need to lie,' she told me softly, 'I know what you're thinking, so you may as well come clean.'

'Oh Primrose, my flower-girl,' I said, pulling her to me, 'please don't be annoyed, I can't bear it. You know I'd do anything to make you happy.'

'Yes, I know you would, Alex,' she said, gently pushing me away and looking up into my eyes, 'and that's why I'm asking you, begging you, to find us another place. Something bad happened here – a murder: I hear screaming, I sense an evil presence, a darkness obscuring the light.'

'Well, obviously we can't go on like this, flower-girl,' I said. 'You're too sensitive to everyday noise, that's the trouble. Why don't we make an appointment with the quack – see what he makes of it?'

'Oh, Alex! You think it's my imagination. You won't accept I'm clairvoyant.'

'No, darling, as much as I love you, I can't believe that. What I know of such people is they enjoy their so-called powers; you're too tortured by whatever's going on in your head.'

'Alex, it's when you don't believe me that I'm tortured. You're making me crazy.' Primrose's pale face was stained with tears and her frail body trembled.

'Well, perhaps there's something in it,' I lied, very disturbed by all this carrying on. 'I'll telephone the estate agents tomorrow; a house might be more suitable, if it's not too expensive. I mean, this flat was the first thing we saw.'

The next morning I gave Mr Rothman a week's notice but we were able to move almost immediately into a bijou one-up-one-down cottage tucked away down a cobbled lane in the old part of town. It was so charming, so full of character, that I hoped Primrose would fall in love with it, and also the rent was very cheap.

Primrose did take to the place on sight and set about making it into a real home. There was an inglenook which seemed to fascinate her and she would sit inside it sewing or knitting, fiddling about with her girlish pastimes while I sat by the hearth reading my newspaper, quite content with married life after all.

But all good things must end, and one evening I came home from work to find Primrose in an agitated state on the front doorstep. She fell into my arms gabbling on about a piercing scream echoing down the chimney and nothing on earth would convince her to ever go near that ingle-nook again.

I tried reasoning with her – it's very windy today, that would explain it – but nothing could convince her. 'We'll have to get away from here, Alex,' she moaned.

'But we've only been here two weeks,' I said. 'We can't keep moving on whenever you take a dislike to noises other people accept as part of everyday living.'

'I knew you wouldn't understand,' she sobbed, 'you've never accepted I'm psychic, but I am, I know I am. Something bad happened here, a murder; I feel evil spirits clouding our lives.'

'Primrose – no,' I protested, 'it's your inability to live with certain sounds that's spoiling things, a kind of mental aberration. There's been no murder. I think we should go see the doctor.'

Of course, we never did see the doctor and so it went on, moving from one rented property to the next, never managing to settle for long, always at the mercy of Primrose's fantasies.

Then I had a brainwave: we should purchase a bungalow off-plan! Why hadn't I thought of that before? I borrowed heavily from the bank, and we watched our dream home being built from the footings to the roof on a piece of land that was clean. Surely Primrose wouldn't imagine any restless souls or evil spirits wandering about in a property with no history! It would be a fresh start for us and we both felt happier at the prospect.

We had been joyfully installed in the new bungalow for only a week when I arrived home to find Primrose waiting for me at the front gate. 'Oh, Alex,' she gibbered, 'I heard a scream from the small bedroom, a blood-curdling scream – like someone being murdered!'

'Darling flower-girl,' I said, hiding my despair in view of her evident distress, 'let's go and sort this out; I'm sure it was a seagull or children playing up the road.' Hand in hand we went inside, Primrose holding back at arm's length. *This is too much*, I thought. *What on earth is going to happen to us? We can't go on like this, can't just move on now we've bought the place.*

I pushed open the door of the small bedroom and peered carefully around. 'Well, there's nobody here, my flower-girl, absolutely nothing to see – have a look for yourself.'

Primrose yanked her hand away roughly. 'Get off me, you stupid *bastard*,' she shrieked, 'don't bloody *patronise* me, OK?'

'Darling, calm down,' I gasped, shocked to my very soul. 'I've never seen you like this. Look – I'm going to make an appointment with Dr Jones. I'll ring him right now, this very minute.' I was turning to go, when Primrose sprang at me, yelling obscenities, her nails clawing at my neck. I grabbed her thin arms and tried to pin them by her sides, endeavouring to protect myself without hurting her, but Primrose, in her madness, was strong. She flung me away and came at me again, her white face a twisted mask of hatred.

But fear gave me strength, and I bound her to me in an iron embrace. It was then she screamed – like someone being murdered, a sound that turned my blood to ice. She jerked violently from side to side in a frenzied attempt to break free, and I tightened my grip around her chest, trying to stop the screaming, crushing the breath from her frail body. It was then I felt something give: there was a crack, a terrible sound of splintering – and that glorious cloud of ash blonde hair slumped sideways, a flower on its broken stem.

Then it was that I began to understand; the scream – of course, it had been her own: an echo from the future…

ALL DUE RESPECT

It showed total lack of respect on Iain's part, turning up tipsy at his late wife's funeral. And that awful Sally, all heaving cleavage, holding him up in case he slithered feet first into the grave-space – she shouldn't wear such a small hat with a chin like hers.

Of course, it was all meant to be a low-key affair, the funeral, bearing in mind Vera's violent mode of departure from this earthly plane. It was never intended it should be a celebration of her life, not when she'd tried to strangle herself with one of Iain's ties and then, when that failed, gulped down some weed-killer, and finally flung herself down the stairs.

Poor Vera was obviously telling us she was not a happy bunny and yet the coroner gave a verdict of accidental death! It was the fall that killed her, apparently, plus there was no evidence to show she had jumped off the top landing; she could quite simply have tripped on the hem of her long negligée. I suppose the coroner knows what he's doing but I have my doubts even though these people *are* highly trained.

Actually, looking back, I had warned Vera about wearing those ridiculous high-heeled mules going up and down the stairs – it was a tragedy waiting to happen. With all due respect, and I regret speaking ill of the dead, Vera was a very vain woman.

It was the milkman, Mr Spalding, who found Vera. He'd eventually noticed how the milk bottles were gathering on the doorstep, peered through the letterbox and there she was sprawled on the hall carpet – neck broken – been there three days. I had been due to meet her later that morning, so you can imagine how stunned I was to hear the terrible news because, although she was down in the dumps, I would never have guessed to what extent. She always managed to paint on a smiling face, did old Vera. Wore far too much makeup for my taste, though, but I never said. And Mr Spalding finding her body just went to prove how long it was since Iain had bothered to go home to his wife.

Of course, Iain gets the house now irrespective of the contents of Vera's will – it was in joint names, you see, so it goes to the survivor – and that awful Sally confirmed his alibi when they were questioned by Det Sgt Hook.

Still, some of us remain very suspicious of the circumstances surrounding her sad demise. It just didn't seem Vera's style. She would never have taken poison of any kind as she hated the thought of being sick, couldn't stand the sight of vomit. Such a squeamish person – good thing she never had a baby to care for.

I've actually known Vera for years. We were at school together. She was my bridesmaid and I was hers. And I knew when she got engaged to Iain it would not be a marriage made in Heaven, but would she listen? Oh, no.

'Judith,' she would say to me, 'Iain and I are on the same plane. We have the same interests. We *do* things together.' And in response to my arched eyebrow, she would continue happily, 'for instance, last evening *I* baked his favourite biscuits while *he* sat at the kitchen table and read the paper.'

Well, how could I argue with that cosy logic? However, as I mentioned previously, no offspring appeared and Vera never said why, only that they had "emotional issues to deal with".

Vera's sister Barbara turned up at the church, sat at the back and, may I say, those bright red trousers with matching peplum jacket really weren't suitable and showed a lack of respect on such a sedate occasion. I saw some of the mourners whispering and looking askance in her direction.

After the brief service Barbara cornered Bob, the village gardener/handyman, a darkly handsome chap who likes to know everybody's business and who, by the way, still hasn't repaired my fence although I paid him up front two weeks ago. I wondered what she was saying to him, quite animated she was. There's something going on, I'm sure.

I noticed Bob was still in his tight jeans and open shirt. I've never seen him wear anything different even in the depths of winter. Surely he could have made an effort for Vera's funeral. Even a second-hand suit from Oxfam would have showed a bit more respect for the deceased.

Apart from Bob, Barbara spoke not one word to anyone else. She even cold-shouldered Reverend Parkinson, although that didn't really surprise me as he was kitted out in a disgusting gravy-stained cassock, being his usual smarmy self, displaying his enormous teeth in *such* a wide grin, a facial expression totally inappropriate and lacking in respect for such a sad event. Someone should take him aside, tell him not to spray spittle when he speaks. But *I'm* not the one to do it, oh no; I'm far too soft hearted to raise the subject face to face. I may send him an anonymous letter, though, and plan to work on that one when the dust has settled.

And Det Sgt Hook was still sporting his workaday anorak! I ask you! Surely these policemen have routine procedures to follow, certain standards laid down for attending particular functions and showing due respect in their line of duty? A smart jacket wouldn't have been too difficult to arrange, I'm sure.

But his attendance at the funeral does beg the question: why is he here, still sniffing around, asking questions, scribbling in his little notebook?

Before the proceedings commenced, I saw him engaged in an earnest conversation with Mrs Trimble, the landlady at Grasson's Hotel. Hotel, she calls it, but it's really only a village pub with sawdust on the floor.

That awful Sally works there, dressed like a tart and calling herself the hotel receptionist but I happen to know otherwise, having seen her pulling pints and collecting empties and occasionally sweeping the flagstones.

I wonder whether Det Sgt Hook noticed Mrs Trimble's false eyelashes. Well, he could hardly have missed them, really, flapping away in his face – they must have caused quite a draught. Honestly, they look so common on her middle-aged face and showed a lack of respect towards Vera, but then, she is only a glorified barmaid when all is said and done. People like her have no sense of decorum.

After the coffin had been lowered into the cold ground and the Reverend Parkinson had droned and intoned a bit more, we walked, dry-eyed, in a straggle to the village hall where I had gone to a great deal of trouble organising the wake, with the usual funerary refreshments laid on plus a nosebag for Mr Spalding's horse, Claudius. I was disappointed to see that neither Mr Spalding nor Claudius had smartened up for the occasion.

But before I could give it much thought or even make an announcement or give a speech, Barbara and Mrs Trimble began to stuff their faces at the buffet, and Iain made straight for the liquor with Sally teetering along behind. How either of them remained upright, I do not know!

Some People

By the way, a very important point I simply must mention: for this extremely sad event *I* wore the minimum of makeup, i.e. a touch of eyeliner and a hint of lipstick; I chose my outfit with the greatest of care, opting for a tasteful tailored costume in black silk crepe over a white Guipure lace blouse with a fascinator of black osprey feathers in my hair. My shoes were black leather courts with a medium heel, and I carried a matching clutch bag.

You see, Vera was my best friend, and *I*, for one, was determined to show her all due respect.

SECRETARY BIRD

'So – you'd like to be my secretary,' said Algernon Comstock. 'I'm assuming you can type?' He was leaning back in his director's chair, his eyes hovering somewhere between my chin and midriff.

I couldn't help noticing how the morning sunshine glinted on the gold watch-chain stretched across his pinstriped waistcoat. His furrowed forehead glistened with perspiration as he stroked his toothbrush moustache with index finger and thumb. I felt tongue-tied, I wasn't used to dealing with such elderly men on a daily basis – I mean, Mr Comstock can't have been a day under forty-five.

Glancing down at the form on his desk, he added, 'OK, we'll take that as read, the job's yours subject to three months' probation, er, what was your name again, ah Miss um Pilbeam. You can start on Monday, Miss er um; take your details to Personnel, good morning.'

My first week at Comstock & Lundquist whirled by in the blur of a new job, getting to grips with my new surroundings, coping with the other secretaries, unapproachable glamour girls all, and working against the clock – 'It's not that complicated,' Mr Comstock retorts when demanding the impossible.

I have learned not to speak unless spoken to, merely offering the ghost of a smile as he is prone to flying off the handle at any hesitation or indecision due to my lack of experience. 'Just do it,' he barks.

So, I sit at my desk fielding telephone calls – 'I'm afraid Mr Comstock is on the other line – may I take a message?' – greeting clients, creditors and salesmen, protecting Mr Comstock's integrity from being questioned, deflecting all criticisms from his enemies and rivals, projecting a wholesome clean-cut image of my boss who is "in a meeting at the moment".

In the meantime, I'm typing urgent letters, important tenders, preparing legal documents, sending emails, receiving emails, keeping the diary, doing the post, and maintaining my smile at all times while expecting to be dismissed at a moment's notice.

Mornings, I take in Mr Comstock's coffee and biscuits on the dot of 10.30. He will glance up briefly with absent-minded disdain. 'Thank you, Miss, er, um,' he says and carries on with his important work of doing The Sun crossword.

And here I am, sitting at my desk when he rings through, ordering me to buy this and that, instructing me to cancel appointments with the dentist, the physiotherapist, his personal trainer, the golf club, his children. 'Time is money, Miss, er, um,' he intones.

So, I browse through online catalogues, choosing flowers, cards and gifts for his wife, his mistress, his kids, using his credit cards while he sits in his office carousing with other members of the board who tell me to say they are "in conference".

I do everything in my power to please him, but still he complains: harrassing, nagging, griping, snapping, holding back from signing the post to make me late leaving the office, and I can discern instant dismissal looming on the horizon.

On a regular basis, I'll do the filing: index cards, Word documents, my fingernails, and occasionally I'll book a hairdresser's appointment for myself (naughty, naughty), whilst keeping an eye on him through the glass partition, watching him cooking the books, humming and smiling smugly to himself at his own trickery and deceit.

And now I sit at my desk, bemused. 'I'm doubling your salary,' he says, handing me one perfect orchid in a cellophane box tied with a silken ribbon. 'You've passed your three-months' probation.'

I gulp in disbelief. 'Well, thank you, Mr Comstock,' I say, lowering my eyes to gaze at his watch-chain, as he stares at my blouse.

Waving away my garbled gratitude, he adds, 'and as a special treat, I've booked us in for lunch at the Grand Atlantic – in one of their private suites, you know, so it can be our little secret. No, don't pretend to be so surprised – you and I have an affinity.'

I lick my lips nervously – what is this affinity of which he speaks? I'm a poor little rabbit caught in the headlights. Huh, think girl, think! Double pay instead of the sack – but at what cost? Will it just be a celebratory lunch or the thin end of the wedge? I'm going mad, what shall I do? Decisions, decisions! Oh, well, what the hell…

Now he's leering at me over the desk. 'There's that come-hither smile again,' he says, 'you little minx! I've seen how you look at me, you're such a wicked lady! Now, let's get this show on the road – yes, that's right, cancel all my appointments for the rest of the day, and now let's see, what was your first name? Come again? Oh, yes – uhu – Petronella. I can hardly go on calling you Miss, er, um outside the office, now can I? Well, Petronella, get a move on then, chop chop. Oh, and by the way, er, can I call you Pet? Yes? Oh that's great – and you can call me Al.'

PRESENTLY

I *am* very efficient! Good at forward planning, you could say. There's only the festive food to get in now, but I can order that online, no problem.

I bought my Christmas cards months ago, in the January sales actually, all the holy ones – they *are* cheaper, and I'm fairly sure I have *all* the presents I need – just have to sort out which is which and make absolutely sure no-one has been left off my list.

For instance – let me write this down – I can give all this smelly stuff, bath salts, soap and shower gel to my numerous female cousins. I hardly ever see them so it won't matter a jot if they're not too thrilled. And what's this body custard all about? I could let Brenda have that as my little joke! Being quite a greedy and stupid creature, she'll eat it, hopefully. Now that would make all this Christmas nonsense really worthwhile.

I think perhaps Gwendoline could make good use of this facial scrub – I've never seen such spotty skin on a woman well into her twenties. Oh, and a leg wax kit would not go amiss either. There, that's two presents just for her – she shouldn't have cause to complain although I'm afraid the girl will moan however one tries to please her and she's bound to think I'm dropping some sort of hint. Tough!

Now these leather driving-gloves are quite nice. Pity I'm a dedicated non-driver otherwise I'd keep them for myself. Maybe they could go to one of the girls at the office – they all have their own cars of course – no wonder the world is warming up at a rate of knots; people don't walk enough these days – they'll lose the use of their legs if they don't watch out, as I never tire of telling them. They just glare and tell me to keep *this* out! But my back is broad, so I take no notice and keep right on dishing out sensible advice. You have to laugh!

Anyway, this ice-cream maker could be quite useful for Patricia's bottom drawer – the silly thing is getting married in the spring. She won't listen to my advice, says I'm a cynical dried-up old faggot (she's kidding of course, as it's common knowledge that no-one is more broad-minded than me). Perhaps I'll throw in this £5 Waterstone's token – it can go towards a self-help book on "How to Submerge Your Own Personality and Keep Your Man Happy"! Hmm!

I have lots of girlie stuff here but not so much for the boys. Perhaps George could have this bottle of red wine although I shouldn't encourage him – he likes boozing, in fact it's his hobby, that and sex. I'm wondering too whether he'd like this bottle of sauternes although it's probably a bit sweet for male taste-buds. But really, come to think of it, he'll drink anything given the chance, the purple-nosed old devil!

Here's a pair of socks in violent red that young Jamie would like. In fact it's a pity they match as he's taken to wearing odd socks, the more garish the better, plus safety pins all over his jacket. I expect any day now to see one stuck through his nose. He tells his mum that all people over the age of 25 are *boring* and why is he here anyway? He didn't ask to be born, etc, etc. *(oh yawn!)* I'm sure I've got a packet of safety pins in my sewing box – I'll chuck them in too – hopefully he'll pin his lips together – that would keep him quiet for a bit.

And for Jamie's mum, the poor bitch, I've put aside this 3D picture of a galleon in full sail. You can put your finger right through, or so it appears. It's probably Art Deco which I've heard of although admit to knowing nothing about, in spite of being an avid fan of Bargain Hunt and Antiques Roadshow. Jamie's mum likes art and that sort of thing – she's had that picture of a Chinese woman on her wall for years; in fact, it's her most-prized possession.

For Jamie's dad, the cheapskate, I've earmarked this snakeskin wallet which is, in truth, quite small but will be just the thing for a man who never stands his round. It also reeks of old tobacco. But, as a dedicated smoker, he won't notice that.

And now for Gran. These dark chocolates in a lavish box look awfully expensive. She'll be thrilled with those, and her eyes are so bad she won't notice they're out of date. They won't do her any harm – she's a tough old bird to have lived to 92, and stale confectionery ain't going to see her off in a hurry. Gran loves handbags so I'll throw in this one in Italian leather – the label does say "made in China" in very small lettering but she won't notice unless she uses her magnifier on it which, knowing her sly ways, she may well do, the old bat. But never mind, it's the thought that counts.

So let's see – a tin of Tartan shortbread always goes down well with the wrinklies, so perhaps cousin Shirley would like this, not that she'll share them round, the selfish pig.

Oh, here we are; my neighbour Mrs Greenstock does like titivating – it seems to be her main pastime, always has her head stuck in the hall mirror checking her appearance, so hopefully these rolled-gold earrings won't turn her lobes green too soon.

Also, I think I'll give her this lipstick in a shade of puce I would never be seen dead in; in fact, it will enhance her corpse-like appearance with all that white face-powder she uses. Anyhow, it'll make her happy!

And now for my coup d'etat (not sure that's the correct phrase but you get my drift)! Yes, the icing on the cake – Aunt Jenny's present. She has her airs and graces, I'm afraid; tries to be so-o-o genteel and goes on ad nauseam about the time she met Princess Margaret.

Without pausing for breath, Aunt Jenny will plunge on and describe in the minutest detail what HRH was wearing, although she could never remember what it was HRH said, except that HRH was extremely gracious, very ladylike but with a faint lingering odour of stale tobacco which was, apparently, quite endearing on such a high-born royal personage.

So, you'll be wondering what I've chosen for Aunt Jenny? It's a coffee table book of Camilla Parker-Bowles! The perfect gift for a crashing snob.

Gosh, I think that's all for today, my knees are killing me, the dust getting in my throat. Still got the garden tools, tiger feet slippers, a furry snood, Wicked Willie coffee mug, fondue set and adult joke book to allocate. I think perhaps they might fit the bill for Shawn, Pauline, Valerie, Carol, Pete and that *filthy swine* Eddie.

So, I'll be back up here tomorrow to finish off my list for another year and, once again, I haven't spent one brass farthing.

There's only one drawback to this method of Christmas present-giving - I have to be damn sure I don't give you back the one you gave me.

OK, folks, that's all for the present(s)!

PRETTY BIRD

They were married, but not to each other, the bank manager and the usherette. He had first noticed Sheree with a jolt to his heart as she guided him down the aisle of the Odeon Cinema with aid of her big torch. Gerald Snetterton did not usually like going to the pictures but he'd been obliged to take his wife Gertrude to see The Seven Year Itch; Gertrude loved the idea of Hollywood glamour but continued to play it safe with twinset and pearls and tightly-permed hair.

Once settled in their seats, Mr Snetterton kept craning his neck, trying to see if he could spot the blonde object of his desire. He left his seat during the film several times, ostensibly to visit the gents' lavatory and, once, to his joy, he managed to come close to her; she smiled automatically, but in reality was staring straight over his head as she was fully six inches taller.

'What's the matter with your waterworks tonight?' Gertrude Snetterton grated, nudging him sharply after he returned from his fourth trip. 'You want to have more self-control!'

'Sorry, dear,' he whispered. 'I shouldn't have had that second glass of wine...' But his excuses were drowned by a chorus of shushing from other patrons in the vicinity.

On the way home, Gertrude fashioned a knot with her lips before expressing her concern more volubly. 'You want to see Dr Chipstead with that bladder of yours, it could be incurable prostate trouble.'

'Never mind, dear,' her husband replied testily, swerving to avoid a stupid pedestrian on a zebra crossing, 'you're well provided for if I pop off suddenly.'

'Oh, don't be so flippant, Gerald,' she tutted. 'When you wake up dead, you'll know I was right, as I always am.'

'Over *your* dead body, you ugly old hag,' he growled under his breath.

But Gerald Snetterton could think of only one thing – Sheree, the blonde usherette, his pretty bird. And so he became a film fan, visiting the Odeon as often as possible without raising the suspicions of his wife or colleagues. Sometimes the object of his desire was on duty, other times not. Gradually, he worked out her roster.

Gertrude Snetterton vaguely noted her husband's distracted mood but was not really too worried as she had a full diary of interests to hold her attention. She belonged to a creative writing class and a poetry society, and had recently begun instruction in line-dancing, plus there was talk of perhaps joining a bird-watching group. None of these pastimes lasted very long but there were always more in the pipeline waiting to be sampled. Gertrude bragged proudly to her circle of acquaintances about her butterfly mentality.

One afternoon when Gerald had slipped out of the office on some pretext or other in order to attend a matinée, he managed to engage the beautiful usherette in conversation. As he introduced himself, Sheree's normally dull eyes lit up when it became evident that Gerald was the manager of the South West Bank and, readily accepting his offer of a coffee after her afternoon shift, she admitted to having maybe noticed him before.

It was a glowing and anticipatory Gerald who found himself sitting opposite Sheree in the café listening to her tale of woe. She was married to Joe, a sailor who was away for most of the year and, naturally, she often felt lonely. Gerald related his sad tale in return, how his wife didn't understand him and how she was more interested in her artistic pursuits and extra-mural activities than in her husband. Then he stopped talking about himself and added, 'I hope you don't mind my observing, but you are the most gorgeous girl I've ever… You put Marilyn Monroe in the shade.'

'Oh Gerald, that the nicest fing anyone's ever…' Sheree giggled, tapping her cigarette with one finger and fiddling with the plastic beads at her neck with the other, 'you are the kindest man I've ever…'

'I was just about to invite you to an art gallery,' he said, touching her arm across the table.

'Oh, was you, dearie?' she replied, fluffing her hair and gazing into space.

'Yes, the Tate, actually. Do you like art?'

'Beg pardon, oh, I've never thought about it,' Sheree said, frowning and blowing smoke from the side of her mouth.

'Music, then,' he suggested. 'Do you like Puccini's operas or maybe you prefer Verdi?'

'Beg pardon, dearie, you've lost me there,' Sheree said, giggling and coughing. 'I don't fink I've ever… Can you talk proper, please?'

'I could let you have some books – on art and music and suchlike – would you like that, Sheree?'

'Beg pardon, oh, er, yes, course I would, Gerald. Anything to please such a kind person… You're the most interesting man I've ever...'

'I could bring them round to your place,' he said quickly, 'where exactly do you live?'

He took the books to her cramped flat that evening where she had prepared a cod's roe curry especially for the occasion.

'I'm sorry, Sheree,' he said, thinking on his feet, 'I've already eaten, and there's no need to cook for me in future, my pretty bird – just a cup of tea will suffice.'

Before long, Gerald was visiting the flat regularly. 'Our love nest,' he said. 'Lucky me, with the prettiest bird in the tree.'

'Oh, you're the kindest, most generous man I've ever…'

Before long, Sheree left her job at the Odeon Cinema and for the next twelve months spent her days shopping and smoking, and, in the evenings, entertaining Gerald and/or trying to improve her mind. At first, Gerald was charmed by her naiveté and her childlike ways. 'Now, darling, did you manage to make a start on that book about The French Impressionists?'

'Hmm? Well, I did flick through the pictures – huh, what a mess – why didn't them painters just buy a camera and take photographs instead? Oh, beg pardon, I did pick out the written bits about brothels and that – them artists, they were a randy lot, wasn't they, Gerald?'

'Yes, my pretty bird, they most definitely were extremely, er, randy – now come over here and sit on my lap...'

At time went on, Gerald Snetterton began to be slightly irritated by her ignorance and her childish ways. 'Oh Sheree, you just don't get it, do you?'

'No, Gerry, I don't; I told you I was dim and you'd never improve my QI.'

'IQ, you mean,' snapped Gerald. 'My God, you can't even get that right, but look, never mind, come over here and sit on my lap…'

Then one evening, without warning, Sheree demanded to be taken out. 'I'll go crazy stuck here in this bloody flat every night. You said in the beginning we was going to paint the town red and stuff, but all you do is bring me frigging books to read and that boring music you can't even tap your foot to. It's like being back at school.'

'But darling, it's good to try and improve our minds; we only use a third of our brains, you know.'

'Well, I'd rather go out to nightclubs and discos and that, and anyway I've never got through a whole book in my life.'

'If you tried harder, my pretty bird…'

'Oh, sod that, Gerry – I'm fed up of it – you're hiding me away like you was ashamed of me.'

'You know my position, Sheree – we can't have people spotting us together.'

'Beg pardon, Gerald – in that case, you should divorce that ugly old wife of yours and marry me; I've waited long enough. Joe's on pins an'all, waiting for you to pay him off so's he can go live in Spain, open a bar and that. Me and you could buy our own house and everyfink.'

'That's not fair, darling; I don't believe Gertrude could be described as old: she's a year younger than myself.'

'Beg pardon, Gerald, I've seen her on them bloody boring holiday snaps you showed me and she's a bleedn' old frump, a right dog – all I can say is woof-woof-woof!'

'Look, darling, you're being unkind and, anyway, Gertrude's appearance doesn't come into this, because – well, at any rate, she would take me for every penny and I'd lose my promotion to Regional Office with all the resulting scandal…'

'Cor, facking 'ell, Gerry! Put one of them boring records on and get your bleedn' violin out…'

'Darling, keep it down: your voice is getting shriller by the second, and please don't keep using that kind of language – it doesn't become you.'

'Whatchoo mean, it doesn't become me? Cor bleedn' 'ell – you come strollin' in 'ere, talking a load of freakin' cowclap…'

'Well, put it another way – you shouldn't demean yourself by speaking in such a vulgar manner. How can I improve your mind when you insist on sounding off like a street walker?'

'That's how you bloody treat me, so what do you bloody expect? And, anyway, what does "demean" mean?'

'It means, ah, what's the use – just come over here and sit on my lap; let's kiss and make up.'

'Oh, keep your filthy paws to yourself; I'm not in the mood. Honestly, Gerry, this is driving me freakin' nuts – but, to tell the trufe, what *I* fink is that all *you* fink about is money and power.'

'No, I don't – that's simply not the case! I fink – I mean, I think about you and me. We have each other, our love, our fantastic sex-life.'

'Cuh, get him,' she said, addressing the wall, 'fantastic, he says – well, it looks pretty facking boring from where I'm sitting, in fact you're the worst lover I've ever…'

'Calm down, my pretty bird, you're angry, you're trying to hurt me – you always say how I turn you on.'

'Well, it was a bleedn' *lie* – you're the oldest, shortest, ugliest, most disgusting man I've ever…'

As soon as Gerald killed Sheree, he knew he'd made a mistake. It was just his temper, you see. He should have counted to ten before head-butting her into the fireplace and finishing her off with the poker.

Some People

But Gerald Snetterton was used to adversity; in fact he thrived on it, and he quickly assumed bank manager mode, i.e. cold and calculating. Best thing now would be to hide the body.

He bundled it into a duvet cover and several black plastic bags tied round and round with rope, and waited until dark before dragging his grisly burden outside and into the boot of his car.

By now he had it all worked out, and the following afternoon he drove to a nearby bluebell wood where he pulled the body into the undergrowth and began covering it with leaves and twigs.

However, had Gerald Snetterton paid more attention to his wife's ramblings over the breakfast table, he would have known that the local bird-watching group had chosen that same woodland for their meeting and at that very moment Mrs Gertrude Snetterton was observing him through her powerful, top-of-the-range binoculars from her hide on a low hillock some fifty yards away.

'I say, everyone,' she called to her fellow-twitchers, 'do look – I believe that's my husband the bank manager; what on earth is he up to?'

STANLEY ALL OVER

I have decided to stay in today: my ten thousand steps will have to wait until tomorrow. Of course, it's never ten thousand by any stretch of the imagination although I'm not really sure how far that would be; definitely more than the half-mile downhill to the village shops and back if I'm being honest and, naturally, if it's raining, I'll take the car.

But even the shortest walk affords me the comforting feeling of coming home again; I do enjoy that enormously, coming home. I love my house. It perches on the hill overlooking Quagmire Village, so goodness knows why my late husband saw fit to name it Morass Manor when Crow's Nest would have been more descriptive of its position.

However, I digress, and this morning I am far too tired for any physical effort after a restless night listening out for real or imagined sounds from the cellar, although I know from experience that the distraction will cease altogether by Friday evening.

Although only in my forties, I am self-sufficient, a widow, my poor Stanley having died in a freak accident in that same basement some years ago. I had reported him missing, and it was several days before his body was discovered in the bowels of the house.

Of course no-one expected me to have heard his terrified cries for help, the cellar ceiling and door having been reinforced with steel during World War II as part of air-raid precautions.

But anyway, the cold-hearted old skinflint had been well past his sell-by date so it was a happy release for both of us, and it was fortunate that his lifetime of scrimping and saving had left me very comfortably off, a fact for which I am ever grateful, and I make a point of marking his demise in my own way on each anniversary.

It was seven years ago last night since he died. In accordance with his wishes, his body had been cremated and the ashes scattered down Quagmire Hill

Well – that was Stanley all over!

But I do get lonely sometimes; I'm perfectly normal in that department and absolutely refuse to sit here staring at the wall bewailing my singleton state. At the same time I have to be so careful of these fortune hunters crawling out of the woodwork as virtually every adult male in Quagmire Village has made it his business to try and get a toe under my table. I know what they're up to, and I deliberately shrug off their attentions, very delicately of course – I wouldn't hurt their feelings for the world; I am not a cruel woman.

Friends and neighbours in the village would swear on oath that I am dedicated to my husband's memory. "That Dorothea Loomis, she's never looked at another man since her poor Stanley died so tragically" I imagine them saying, compressing their lips and nodding their heads in sympathy.

I make a point of contributing hugely to village charities and am regularly invited to cut the ribbons at church fetes, that sort of thing. And apparently, our darling Reverend Burgoyne has dubbed me "Queen of Quagmire". I rather like that!

The Reverend is such a sweet man and recently acknowledged my obvious piety by inviting me to train as a lay reader. What a compliment! I am quite tempted to accept the challenge especially as my appointment would really irritate that ghastly woman Marjorie Seligman; she is the only female verger at our church and insists on wearing her robes of office at all times, even when not on duty. I'm afraid that Marjorie is not always Christian in her attitude, particularly towards members of her own sex. But I do my best to overcome her narrow-minded jealousy by including her in the conversation whenever we are in Reverend Burgoyne's earshot.

In fact, please excuse my immodesty when I admit to being a people-pleaser, a leading light in Quagmire, quite a pillar of the community. I help out at the school and also the library whenever possible, subject to my regular village and church engagements.

But if I feel the need for a different sort of company, I'm not afraid to go out and mingle some evenings. I take my car away from the village environs and into the city where no-one knows me.

Those singles bars are a real eye-opener, an education. It's fascinating to watch the games people play, see how they interact and flirt, and it's a pastime of mine to identify the likely victims and their abusers.

You could describe me as a people-watcher. I have no difficulty striking up a conversation with someone who catches my eye. The target doesn't have to be handsome or attractive – even interestingly repulsive will suffice – in fact, they are the most grateful ones, quite frankly.

And the greedy ones believe they've landed on their feet meeting a rich widow like me. They think they can make a killing, that I'll be putty in their hands, a pushover; hah, I can't help laughing up my designer sleeve as I reel in a likely subject.

I never use my own name: and therefore I've been variously known as Sheila, Kate, Vanessa, Lizzie, Diane, Sharon and Joyce. For for further security and anonymity, I try to alter my appearance for each new relationship with wigs, clothes and makeup. Great fun!

But to be fair on myself (please don't run away with the wrong impression), I only ever see one man at a time – I am what you might call a serial monogamist, faithful in my own way, and never a two-timer: *that* would be quite immoral in my book.

And because all this nocturnal activity is kept separate from my village life, a current boyfriend is asked back to Morass Manor only under a certain circumstance, that is, on my poor Stanley's anniversary.

Under cover of darkness it's an easy matter to tempt an admirer back here for a night of socialising, lightheartedly persuading him to leave his car behind with the promise of a lift back next morning.

You can imagine how eager these fellows are to accept my invitation, fair straining at the leash, one would say. Then I give the chosen one a good time, invite him to partake of my lavish food and drink, plus other comforts, and only later do I offer a conducted tour of the wine cellar as a special treat.

To a man, they have gone willingly and eagerly down those uneven stone steps into the dank, dark, mouldering oubliette below. Not one of them appears to have been warned by the overwhelming foul stench as I open the door and smilingly invite entry across the threshold.

Oh, it's all too easy! And one would never guess how impervious that reinforced steel door is, once slammed shut. But I have to sometimes wonder what the conditions are like down there; I've never had the inclination to check (I am rather squeamish if I'm being truthful), but I can imagine it's probably no picnic for the new arrival.

Now, I realise some of you will accuse me of being a black widow; but in my own defence I have to state that I don't hold with unnecessary killing, oh, no, and normally I wouldn't hurt a fly, but the business must be done and someone has to do it!

For, *ladies*, have you noticed how the most unattractive of men will offer advice on how to improve your appearance; and the really stupid ones expect you to shut up and listen? Well, that was Stanley all over…

I rest my case!

FRANKLY SPEAKING

MAUDE: I sat with old Frank at the bingo last night
What a nerve, he held onto my knee

EDNA: No, I think you're mistaken, that cannot be right
He doesn't like you, he likes me!

MAUDE: Well, he asked me to go to the pictures with him
There's a musical on, what a prank

EDNA: No, you're likely mistaken, that must have been Jim
He does a good imitation of Frank

MAUDE: I know you're just jealous, but I am in lust
And I think old Frank loves me as well

EDNA: No – I'd like to save you from biting the dust
There's tales of old Frank I've heard tell

MAUDE: But what did you hear of so charming a man
It can't have been much of a chiller

EDNA: Well – where did he get so alarming a tan?
In Spain – he's a serial killer

MAUDE: Oh, you mean he's a murderer out on the loose?
Why did you not tell our Miss Beagle?

EDNA: I meant lady-killer – you silly old goose
They can't touch you for that, it's still legal

MAUDE: So you're saying he likes all the ladies – OK
I'll love taming this frisky old guy

EDNA: But his red nose is glowing, he likes his rosé -
And his red, and his white, sweet, or dry

MAUDE: So what are you saying – that he is a boozer?
I think he just likes a good time

EDNA: I fear you'll find out that old Frank is a loser
And please never lend him a brass dime

MAUDE: So what are you saying – that he likes to gamble?
I know he likes horses as pets

EDNA: You've heard of that song 'Oh didn't he ramble'?
And the saying 'Please place no more bets'?

MAUDE: If it's only the gee-gees then I'm not too fussy
An animal lover I like

EDNA: No, it's horses and dogs and casinos, you hussy
You should tell Frank "just get on yer bike"

MAUDE: So you're saying he fritters his money away
Which is *why* he owes *me* quite a lot

EDNA: Yes, spongers like him have the Devil to pay
I wouldn't like you to land in a spot

MAUDE: Well it's not in the hundreds – it's just a few quid
I shouldn't have opened my trap

EDNA: Hmm, he's an undischarged bankrupt, his real name is Sid
And Customs are closing the gap

MAUDE: So you're saying that Frank, I mean Sid, is a smuggler
What else are you telling me now?

EDNA: He's a jailbird, a con-man, old lag, and a juggler
He'll cook the account books, and how!

MAUDE: So, an embezzler then, is what you're suggesting
I know Frank is clever at sums

EDNA: He's too calculating, and always divesting
Of cash, one who easily succumbs

MAUDE: Oh, I'm not going to *listen* to all these dire warnings
Frank and I plan on taking a trip

EDNA: Hmm, *you'll* wake up sadder, one of these mornings
Don't say you weren't given the tip

MAUDE: So you're saying that Frank is a bringer of doom
I need proof, not a few words of warning

EDNA: He was seen creeping out of a resident's room
At seven o'clock in the morning

MAUDE: But Frank is a livewire, enjoying a revel
I know he's lived life to the full

EDNA: Oh my dear, please take care, he's a randy old devil
And will always be there – on the pull

MAUDE: Whatever you say won't detract me from him
And in fact makes my yearning grow stronger

EDNA: Yes, some silly dames go right out on a limb
But you won't feel this way for much longer

MAUDE: Oh, last evening at dinner old Frank was so charming
He insisted on sitting adjacent

EDNA: You misunderstood Frank, he can *be so* disarming
I advise do not be so complaisant

MAUDE: He invited me back to his bedsit just then
I would guess *you* were never that sporty

EDNA: Well, I was – and I am – he gets eight out of ten
With detention all night for being naughty!

PERFECT PITCH

'Come on, who's been at my marmalade again,' I growled. 'It's gone half an inch below the mark.'

'Don't look at me, duckie – it must have been one of the French girls,' Jayne said from the depths of her armchair, generous cleavage bursting forth, charm bracelets jangling, as she painted her toenails scarlet whilst humming a tune excruciatingly off-key.

It had been obvious from the outset that she had cloth ears beneath that long dark hank of hair. The girl was definitely tone-deaf. I never knew what she made of our regular visits to sweaty, smoky jazz-clubs: even the earthy beat could not penetrate her thick skull because she had no sense of rhythm either. But in spite of that, an eager succession of dancing partners queued up for her attentions, especially in the slow numbers. I couldn't understand it myself.

But she did enjoy her attempts at singing, and would happily warble the wrong words to popular songs as we played housekeeping in our shared flat in one of Soho's cobbled side streets.

'No, it's not Killarney,' I would laugh, disguising any slight irritation, 'it's Dakota – take me back to the Black Hills of Dakota.'

'You're too pernickety, a perfectionist to a fault,' she would say. 'Details aren't important. It's my own interpretation that counts.' And on she would go.

It went further than just singing the wrong words or being off-key with no sense of rhythm: I tried to get her to read literature for a change, but she stuck faithfully to her women's magazines, trying out the new fashions and makeup, washing out her little white cotton gloves of an evening, plastering her face in cream at bedtime, hoping to greet the world spick and span each morning. The romantic short stories by the likes of Barbara Cartland enthralled Jayne. 'Life's not like that,' I remarked. 'Life is a serious matter. You shouldn't believe all that twaddle.'

'Oh you're an old stick-in-the-mud – loosen up a little,' she would say good-humouredly flicking through Woman's Own, grating my nerves with her personal version of St Louis Blues.

'A little self-improvement never comes amiss,' I chivvied. 'Perhaps if you had more interesting subjects to discuss, instead of all the usual empty-headed girlie stuff, you'd get yourself a clever boyfriend like my Rupert instead of all these lads who hang you around at the club. Rupert's an intellectual; he says we have a meeting of minds.'

'What? Don't you ever – you know – kiss each other goodnight?' Jayne smiled, rather slyly.

'Not really,' I shrugged. 'Rupert says we are above all that; our relationship is on a higher plane, based on mutual respect and trust. Do you know, even when I finished The Times cryptic crossword for him, he looked amazed but also pleased in a secret kind of way.'

'Really?' Jayne was frowning now, appearing to concentrate on her toes.

'Yes,' I continued, warming to my theme, 'as well as being a wonderfully sensitive saxophonist, Rupert is a highbrow with an encyclopaedic memory. And, of course, he has an artistic temperament, and so I make allowances for that.'

'Oh, why did she fall for the leader of the band,' Jayne sang tunelessly. 'You always did want to hook a musician. But has he ever taken you out for a meal or anywhere other than seeing you at the club? I don't think so.'

'He doesn't want to put any pressure on me – he's not like the others, he's a real gentleman and, anyway, it wouldn't be fair if I interrupted his artistic flow by using my womanly wiles before he's ready,' said I, blushing.

'You haven't got many of those, Amy dear, and if you had they'd be wasted on him as I think he's probably – well, you know,' Jayne was starting on the other foot as she spoke, her tongue out in concentration. 'Anyway, for a woman pushing 22, you look like a bloody art student. It's not as if you're still at college – you're a common or garden typist in an office, for goodness sake. Why don't you ditch that old grey duffel coat and those scruffy drainpipe trousers for something prettier and more feminine? Start wearing lipstick and rouge. Then perhaps Rupert would change his orientation and be more affectionate towards you.'

I ignored this tirade as we could never agree on these matters. I preferred my pale-lipped, panda-eyed Bohemian look to her red-lipped tarty one. After all, most of our crowd wore duffel coats – it was a sign of our individuality, our artistic tendencies, and furthermore we didn't wish to look like normal run-of-the-mill proles. Had I been born a man, I should have grown a beard.

And Rupert was, of course, my trophy boyfriend. I would stand at the back of the club proudly watching him play, waiting for the interval when I'd put my arm proprietorially through his as the band trooped over to the pub on Charing Cross Road for a twenty-minute break.

He would stand there at the bar, rolling a cigarette, bright eyes darting hither and thither before regarding me from under his eyebrows. He didn't like small talk, preferring to discuss important matters with the other band members, but I didn't mind just being by his side, flushed with success, bathed in reflected glory, conscious of envious glances from the other girls.

Once, he led me to a corner table and we sat down with our drinks. I felt a warm sensation as if we were about to have a cosy chat, but instead he took out a creased copy of The Times from a pocket in his corduroy jacket and proceeded to scan the half-completed cryptic crossword. That was the one occasion I finished it off for him. His eyes flickered and then he laughed, called me a bluestocking, which I took as a compliment, but after that we just stood at the bar in spite of my expectations of further intimate huddles at corner tables.

Rupert said I was the only woman he'd met who had heard of everything he mentioned and therefore he couldn't tell me anything new. 'Thank you, kind sir,' said I, 'that is praise indeed coming from you.'

I tried to kiss him goodnight once, but he gripped my shoulders and held me at arms' length, gazing into my eyes with a serious expression. 'You know what could happen,' he said. 'I'm not the sort to take advantage.'

'Perhaps I'd like you to take advantage,' I retorted, and then thought better of it. 'Oh, sorry, I didn't mean…'

'That's sounds like something your little fat friend would say,' Rupert interrupted with a grimace. 'What's her name – Jean?'

'Oh, don't say that, you awful man – and it's Jayne, not Jean – and she's not fat, just a bit top-heavy, that's all,' I said.

Rupert shrugged. 'She looks like a slag – I can't stand women like her. She could be a bad influence on you if you weren't so intelligent.'

'Oh, you're so perceptive,' I enthused. 'And have you heard her singing? Doesn't it get on your nerves? It gets on mine especially, what with my perfect pitch.'

He said it was patently obvious I could carry a tune, and not many women were capable of that. Praise once again! I was so lucky to have a man who appreciated me.

'But I've never heard anyone as tone deaf as Jayne,' I pursued. 'Don't you agree?'

'She is pretty awful in that department, as well,' he said, his eyes narrowing. He looked so serious that I couldn't help saying, 'a smile takes less energy than a frown,' to which he replied, 'but it takes even less for you not to point it out to me.' And he picked up his pint and swigged it down in one.

The following Saturday, the French girls who shared our large apartment were throwing a party and we began inviting people by the dozen. I asked Rupert to come but he refused on the grounds he had a gig out of town that evening and, anyway, he didn't approve of my "flighty" flat-mates and their friends.

In any event, the party began in earnest at 11 o'clock, and it was swinging by midnight; some guests were staggering drunk and the wonderful array of French cuisine buffet food had early on been pillaged. Jayne, sporting a low-cut jersey top, an ankle chain and stiletto heels, had happily attacked the vodka and was swanning around the men, vamping shamelessly.

Then, inevitably, and to my intense irritation and horror, she stood on the table and began singing "The Black Hills of Killarney" in her usual manner, i.e.

wrong words and off-key. The whole company, apart from myself, roared with glee and joined in.

'Oh, what a row – why does she always have to spoil things,' I was yelling above the din, when I spotted Rupert shouldering his way through the throng. He made straight for Jayne, swung her off the table by her legs, let her slither slowly down to his level and kissed her full on the lips for what seemed like several minutes.

I couldn't believe it! Was he drunk?

'Hey folks – this is one way to stop her noise,' he laughed as they came up for air, and then, gazing at the girl swooning like a rag doll in his arms, he shouted, 'Jayne, you're gorgeous, I fancy you like mad,' and heaving her over his shoulder he carried her off to loud whooping from the crowd.

Well – who had the perfect pitch, and who was off-key?

So much for the higher plane!

REGRETS

I lie on my bed – thinking
Of people I never got round to meeting
The years that were wasted just sitting and eating
Get-rich schemes that turned out self-defeating
I stare at the ceiling – unblinking

I lie on my bed – drowsing
Recalling the times when I spoke out of turn
I'd spend-up just as if I'd got money to burn
Experience a thing that I never did learn
And now it's too late to put right all those years spent carousing

I lie on my bed – devising
Possible ways to make a fresh start
Perchance it could be through a man's heart
But the usual thing is we're poles apart
Tis a far better thing that I stay here alone – fantasising

I lie on my bed – dozing
Pictures of people float by in my head
Some of them living and others are dead
Too late to say sorry, my tears are unshed
My heart feels like stone and the door on my past is now closing

I lie on my bed – dreaming
Of far-away places that I've never seen
How I could have starred upon the big screen
And strange how some people keep calling me Jean
It's all much too much and I stand on the edge of my personal cliff and I'm screaming!

A CHRISTMAS VERSE

That time of year has come round once again
It's shopping for women and boozing for men
Excitement for young ones, nostalgia for old
When will a Christmas ever be undersold?

The shops are just heaving, the food is a chore
And wrapping the presents quite simply a bore
We're all going mental – there's no help because
There ain't no such thing as a Sanity Clause

BREAKFAST TIME
(With apologies to Gershwin's "Summertime")

Breakfast time
And the stomach is queasy
Nerves are jumping
And my feelings run high

Oh, your coffee's cold
And the porridge gone lumpy
I'll boil you an egg
There's no time for a fry

One of these mornings
You'll have to get your own breakfast
You'll be so sorry
When I've decided to fly   *(bye-bye)*

Until that morning
You'll have to eat what you're given
So do me a favour
Wash up and I'll dry

THIRD AGE

How lovely it is to be no longer young
I don't have to wear a stud in my tongue
Nor in my nose, nor in my lip
How free it feels to be so un-hip

I'm never seen wearing a cap back-to-front
Can eschew a tattoo, to be perfectly blunt
I don't have to get drunk, don't have to smoke
I can leave out the spliffs, refrain from the coke

I stay in if I want on a Saturday night
Don't have to hang out, or get into a fight
Need not leave my belly exposed to the breeze
Or wear skirts so short that they'd numb my fat knees

Of these new mobile phones, my ears are kept free
iPods and stereos – and what's this, MP3?
This computer age has left me behind
And I really don't wish to erase and rewind

Maturity is fine, I'll say it once more
A hometruth I should have thought of before
For these golden years have at last come my way
I'm no longer blonde – I'm glad to be grey

BLIND FAITH

Right, said God, we'll do this together
Your life will be fine with no stormy weather
Happiness thine - just for the taking
So come out, start living, a new dawn is breaking
OK, said I, let's give it a shot
It's got to be better than what I have got
It's got to be better than darkness and space
I'd like to join this so-called human race

Yep, said God, you bet, that's right
Be in it to win it, yeah – out of sight
I guarantee thou shalt be a winner
A charmed life awaits this naive beginner
My God, I vowed, my belief is true
I'll come out now and abide in you
As long as you will light my way
And put me right if I should stray

All right! growled God, don't drag your feet
How much more must I entreat
Get a move on, come on down
It's time for you to paint the town
Oh wow, I cried, what joy, what bliss
This chance of life I cannot miss
Bring it on, the game's afoot
God is Good – that's so well put!

But what's this urban neon-lit night?
Why am I poor, in such sad plight?
God said, 'Just kidding - it's my little joke'
And then disappeared in a puff of smoke

NOT YOU

Honest, I mean it, it's not you, it's me
I know I'm the one who's at fault
I'm only concerned for your happiness here
Surely our marriage should come to a halt

Really, I mean it, it's not you, it's me
I know I'm the one out of step
No really, my welfare is just not important
You need someone else who is lively, with pep

Truly, I mean it, it's not you, it's me
I've come to the end of my rope
I can't bear to see you so foolishly happy
Can't you see that for us there is simply no hope?

Quite frankly, I mean it, it's not you, it's me
Everyone says you're a fabulous guy
The life of the party, hail fellow well met
But to live with is boring as watching paint dry

Sincerely, I mean it, it's not you, it's me
I'm holding you back, it's not fair
Of course, people change out of all recognition
Too much for this girl with the delicate air

Oh, all right, I admit it, it's not me, it's you
You're boorish, disgusting, a lout
You will leave the seat up and sleep with your socks on
I'd be glad if you'd simply arrange to move out

NEUTRAL GROUND

So there they sat, the five of them, around a solid wooden table in the Akimbo Arms on the occasion of their Christmas meal, feeling mighty uneasy at the prospect of being in each other's company for this unusual event, together for the first time on neutral ground:

First at the table sat Egbert Wormold, sole practising solicitor in the village of Quagmire, who ran the office "ship-shape and Bristol fashion", as he was fond of saying. His four staff members, all residing local to the office, were paid less than they would have earned commuting to the nearby town of Quorum Thisbé.

Egbert Wormold was tall, thin and grey-faced, and had been married to Ouida Wormold for twenty grim years or more. Their union had not been blessed with offspring, much to their mutual relief, as neither one of them had much patience, least of all with each other. Ouida Wormold, with her laugh like a splintering iceberg, kept herself scrawny through severe and constant dieting; she loved new clothes above anything.

Their home, Mangrove Lodge, was kept spick and span by a daily woman, Mrs Brisket, who also did the weekly food shopping and very often the cooking if Mrs Wormold was too busy with her various activities over in Quorum Thisbé; these included organising an annual fashion show in the town hall which seemed to take up a lot of her time.

Then, to Mr Wormold's right sat Sadie Twerton, a girl of 25 who had joined the firm at 16, was still thought of as the office junior, and who freewheeled to work on her bicycle at Mr Wormold's request as this mode of transportation often came in handy for going on errands or delivering messages.

Next came the general typist, Maureen Sagebrush, a married lady of middle years. All day long she hammered away on her Remington Rand as if pursued by all the furies, speaking only when absolutely necessary, and uttering a polite "thank you" as she received her morning mug of coffee or afternoon tea. Colleagues surmised her marriage was not a happy one although the matter was never mentioned nor discussed. People noticed that Mr and Mrs Sagebrush were never seen together around the village and, in fact, Mr Sagebrush spent many hours in his garden shed well away from the house and, so Mrs Brisket told Mrs Wormold, often slept in there on a truckle bed.

Next to Maureen sat Alfred Beems, the chief clerk, a callow man in his mid-thirties who had grown a moustache and beard in the vain hope of appearing more virile. He had tried to summon up courage to ask Sadie to go to the Roxy Cinema in Quorum Thisbé but she invariably turned away at his approach. He had also wanted to invite her for a drink at the Dogleg Arms which stood only a few doors down from the office, but once again she had avoided being face to face with him. In truth, she was revolted by his facial hair which often retained froth from his coffee or bits of food from his lunchtime sandwich. She could not bear to look at him most of the time but, to her incredulity, no-one else appeared to notice his untidy state.

Finally, on Mr Wormold's left at the table sat Doris Clatworthy, his secretary, a spinster in her late thirties. She was tall, thin, plain, devoted to her boss and wedded to her job; she never took a holiday and often volunteered to work at the weekends during busy periods.

As previously indicated, Egbert Wormold was proud of the fact he ran the office to a strict regime, a *regimented* regime as he termed it, where the workload was dealt with in an efficient manner; the filing was done each morning, the daybook was checked every afternoon at 5 o'clock, and the system of double-entry accounting was balanced to the penny each week.

If a staff member's birthday happened to fall on a weekday, Mr Wormold would send Sadie out to buy cakes from Quidgley's bakery, and at Christmas he allowed a dusty tree to be hauled out of the cupboard and decorated with ancient, peeling baubles. Streamers and paperchains were not permitted as they were deemed to be a fire hazard. The staff were usually awarded a Christmas bonus of two days' pay, which, being included in their wages, was taxed at source. Egbert Wormold was unbending in his adherence to the rules.

This particular Christmas, to everyone's quiet amazement, Mr Wormold had had an announcement to make: 'Attention, everyone – by way of thanking you for an excellent year's results, I am planning a seasonal dinner at the Akimbo Arms – no partners invited; in short, just the five of us! Please turn up on Wednesday evening at 7.30 in your best bib and tucker – and now, back to work.'

Gossip was discouraged in the office and so no discussion of this turn of events developed, but particular members of staff began to dread the intimate meal which loomed ever closer.

Come the day, they assembled in the bar of the Akimbo Arms at 7.30, and Mr Wormold bought the pre-dinner drinks, sweet sherry for the ladies, dry for the men. Then they were led to their table by the waiter, Walter Cleasby, an ex-schoolfriend of Mr

Wormold's, although Mr Wormold always forgot a face and had no memory of him.

So there they sat, the five of them, eyes cast down reading the menu, or glancing surreptitiously this way and that, looking anywhere but at each other. Walter Cleasby did a smooth job of taking their orders but he could plainly discern their discomfiture and so he decided to do them a favour and jolly up the event by spiking their wine.

Halfway through the main course, Mr Wormold was not at all surprised to hear himself announce: 'Did I ever tell you lovely folk that I absolutely loath my wife? And have done since our wedding night when she insisted upon separate bedrooms? She's never been a woman who enjoyed sex and we invariably had to make an appointment about twice a year, if I was lucky.'

'Oh, poor Mr Wormold,' shrieked Doris Clatworthy. ' You know you can always come and share my bedroom any time – preferably tonight?'

'Please call me Egbert,' he replied, taking her hand to kiss it, and gazing deeply into her eyes.

'Well that's nothing,' rejoined Maureen Sagebrush. 'What about my Bert – he's slept in the garden shed for the past ten years. He thinks I don't know he likes wearing a negligee in bed. And he wears a matching ribbon in his long curly wig.'

By this time, Alfred Beems had grasped Sadie's hand across the table to slip a silver napkin ring on her finger. 'Sadie,' he cried, 'you know I love you. Will you marry me?'

'Look, Alfred,' grated the object of his affection, 'I think you should know that you repel me enormously, and also I'm seriously considering turning into a lesbian.' Leaping to her feet to perform a suggestive dance, she added, 'there's a girl works at the bank that I fancy like mad, mmm, phwoar!'

'Oh Doris,' moaned Egbert to his secretary. 'How I wish I had never married Ouida. Please come and sit next to me and I'll tell you all about it.'

Doris Clatworthy swiftly moved into Sadie's vacant chair and crooned, 'Egbert, my darling, how I wish you'd married me instead.'

'Ouida is pure evil,' Egbert continued, oblivious to Doris's impassioned cry, 'she's never been a good wife to me.'

'I'd be a good wife to you,' said Doris, her voice breaking with emotion and her eyes filling with tears. But Mr Wormold did not seem to have heard as he continued with the tale of his unbearable home life. Doris was just happy to sit there beside him, nodding sympathetically, kissing his cheek, her arms around his neck.

Maureen Sagebrush had now broken into loud sobbing with her head in her arms and was comforted by Alfred Beems who joined her in crying his eyes out. Fortunately, there were no other diners in the Dogleg Arms restaurant that evening and so Walter Cleasby was able to watch the proceedings with a great deal of enjoyment, there being only himself and Luigi the chef on duty.

And so the evening progressed into something of an orgy of intimate confessions and confidentialities, pent-up frustrations and tears, Luigi deserting his kitchen to join Walter as a spectator.

'Just look at that lot,' laughed Walter, 'it's what I like to see, people letting their hair down, especially prigs like Egbert Wormold – makes this dead-end job worthwhile.'

At the stroke of midnight, Walter and Luigi called a taxi to ensure that everyone got home in one piece.

All Ouida Wormold said when her husband staggered in with his tie on back-to-front was, 'What time do you call this?'

'I call it fifteen minutes past midnight – what do you call it, you frigid old witch,' Egbert replied, laughing uproariously at his own witticism as he stumbled up the stairs to his lonely bed.

The next morning, everyone turned up at the office on the dot as per usual, Egbert Wormold more grim-faced than usual because of a *strange* headache he could not account for.

Not one of his staff said a word about the previous night's jollifications – and not because gossiping was frowned upon or that they felt hungover – oh no: their silence was simply for the reason nobody remembered a single thing about their evening out together, an evening spent on neutral ground.

PASSING STRANGERS

Even though they both resided in the outskirts of Quagmire Village, Marlene Mottershaw and Horace Meakins had never met, never suspected their lives could be anonymously intertwined and that their respective actions would have far-reaching consequences.

Miss Marlene Mottershaw, a very slim female of 28, was a shop assistant in Branscombe & Wadsworth's department store in the nearby town of Quorum Thisbé; she was employed on the confectionery counter at the busy, noisy, lower ground level, but the girl's ambition in life was to move into ladies' fashions on the first floor. Marlene would have enjoyed entering the elevator each morning, stepping out into the hushed surroundings, helping to dress the elegant mannequins posing on little platforms dotted around the luxuriously carpeted floor.

Horace Meakins had, on the other hand, already achieved his goal in life, which was to be third in command at Goldstrand's Insurance Company at their Quorum Thisbé branch office. Horace's wife, Daphne, had grown bitter and shrewish with frustration. 'Horace Meakins,' she would shrill, 'why aren't you in charge – you've worked at Goldstrand's, man and boy. You're just not assertive enough.'

'I know my place,' was his meek and maddening reply. Daphne took to reading through the "personals" in the local paper in her search for a more masculine companion.

Marlene Mottershaw, the shop-girl, had a boyfriend, one Miles Fosdyke, whom she adored unconditionally. Miles, however, spelling his name

"Myles" with a "y", had signed up with a dating agency in his search for a younger, meatier woman with large breasts. In the meantime he nagged Marlene relentlessly: 'why don't you eat more and put on some weight – I'm sure it can't be healthy to be so skinny.'

'Oh, Miles,' she would reply nervously, fully aware of overt sulky glares aimed in her direction. 'You know I prefer being thin like the models in ladies' fashions. Anyway if I try to eat more, it makes me sick to my stomach.' Marlene stuck a finger in her mouth and pretended to vomit, a procedure which caused her to cough as she was in the throes of yet another cold. She blew her red nose and apologised.

'Well, you could save up and have surgery to improve your chest,' Miles said, frowning, trying to ignore the unlovely sight of Marlene inspecting the contents of her handkerchief. 'It's the least you can do if you want to please me.'

'You know I'm terrified of doctors, Miles,' she whined. 'I'd do anything for you, but to go under the surgeon's knife, I really don't know! Well, I promise I'll think about it, but the savings I've put by are towards our honeymoon in Cornwall.'

Horace Meakins, in another part of the village, had an all-engrossing pastime, which was making collages out of scraps of silk, satin and velvet and decorating them with bits of lace, sequins, beads, feathers, buttons, anything he could find. This particular day, he had almost completed his latest, very large, work of art and needed a little something extra as a finishing touch. He went rummaging through Daphne's clothes hoping to find discarded beads and such in the bottom of her wardrobe. Finding an unfamiliar turquoise satin dress embroidered with pearls, Horace gasped with joy, thinking this little lot would keep him going for months. He gently took it out and held it up to himself in front of the floor-length mirror just as Daphne entered.

'What's this?' she sniffed. 'Trying on my clothes? Changed your orientation, have you?'

'No, dear, I was just…'

'Oh, don't give me that! You still haven't explained those red silk cami-knickers that I found in your coat pocket.'

'I did tell you, Daphne – I got them from a jumble sale – for my collages.'

'Are you sure you're not wearing them under your trousers? Anyway, you and your silly hobby! Why don't you find a more manly way of spending your time than messing about with bits of material, wearing cami-knickers and now trying on my dresses. Stand up for yourself, why don't you, and be a bit more aggressive, more macho: this attitude will never get you promotion at work.'

About the time this was happening, Marlene Mottershaw had an idea of how to improve her chest without resorting to surgery. It came to her in a flash of inspiration. In her lunch break she took the elevator to the second floor of Branscombe and Wadsworth's store and began to browse in the ladies' underwear department. She bought a generously-padded 42D bra festooned with lashings of lace.

'But madam, are you sure you want this?' queried the glamorous assistant, flapping her long false eyelashes. ' I can see it's not your size without getting out my tape measure.'

'Oh, it's for a friend,' lied Marlene. She hurriedly paid for the item and, stowing it into her shopping bag, went on her way rejoicing. That same evening, all excited, she turned up to meet Miles wearing the new bra which she had infilled with paper hankies.

Miles's face was granite-grim as he beheld Marlene carrying all before her, her chest region projecting in an obviously fake manner beyond her unbuttoned coat.

'What on earth have you been doing to yourself? You're a travesty! I can't be seen with you like that,' and he began pulling wads of paper tissue from her cleavage. 'It's a good job it's dark – I don't want people seeing us.'

'Oh, Miles,' cried Marlene, 'I was trying to please you.'

'Well, you haven't,' growled Miles, thinking of a woman he had been in contact with via the dating agency, one who said she was size 38B. 'Look, I think we'd better not see each other for a while, eh? Let things calm down a bit. I'll give you a bell in a week or two.'

'Oh Miles,' wept Marlene, dabbing a sodden tissue at the murky bubble she had just blown through one nostril. 'I didn't think it would upset you. I promise to see a surgeon, get my chest enlarged, just for you.'

'Let's perhaps leave it for now, eh? On the backburner, eh? Cheer up. I'll ring you, OK?'

'All right, Miles, anything you say,' Marlene said from the depths of her paper hankies. 'But aren't you going to say goodnight? Don't I get a kiss?'

'Erm, well, perhaps not, seeing as you have another cold. I don't want to catch it, do I? Anyway, I've got to go now, OK? See you around, eh?' And he was off like a bullet, round the corner to the telephone box where he intended ringing the 24-hour dating agency to fix up a meeting with Miss X.

Marlene went into a ladies' lavatory and took off the huge bra, carelessly stuffing it into her coat pocket. As she walked home towards Quagmire Village crying inconsolably, she rummaged around her person for yet another tissue, and the bra, which had been left half hanging from her pocket, fell out onto the level crossing. Not noticing her loss, Marlene made her way home.

About an hour after this, Horace was returning from work where he had been doing compulsory overtime, and took a short cut via the level crossing. He spied Marlene's bra and, thinking the lace trim was just what he needed to put the finishing touch to his collage, picked it up and put in his briefcase.

When Horace reached home, Daphne was out. Horace left his briefcase on the hall table and went to make himself some supper as there didn't appear to be any evidence of Daphne having cooked him anything. Thirty minutes later Daphne came home, saw a lacy bra strap protruding from Horace's briefcase and began screeching, 'What's this – you, you womaniser – or should I say transvestite!'

'Oh, ha ha, erm, it's not mine, it's not my size – too large for me,' Horace joked weakly.

'Oh, so you've tried it on, then?'

'Don't be silly, Daphne – I found it on the level crossing – it's for my collage.'

'Where? Oh, pull the other one!' she screamed. 'Aargh – this is the last straw, you're a pervert, I've had enough of this, I'm packing and going home to mummy.'

But if the truth were known, Daphne had already planned this course of action, having only that same evening been in telephone contact with a fellow named Myles, spelt with a "y", who seemed a better type of person, more ambitious, more macho.

Horace felt a curious mixture of fear and relief by all this carrying on and decided to make himself scarce until Daphne had moved out, so he walked into the village and found a café in Market Square where he settled himself comfortably with his evening paper at a little table covered with a pink checked cloth.

When Marlene reached home, she realised with a shock that the bra was no longer in her coat pocket. Hoping to obtain a refund on her unwise purchase, she began retracing her steps looking for the undergarment, but there was no sign of it. Sad and empty-handed, she headed back to Quagmire towards Market Square. 'I might as well go into the Pink Teapot Café,' Marlene thought, 'I could do with a cup of tea.' She sat down on a bentwood chair at a little table covered with a pink checked cloth.

There was only one other customer in the café, a nice man, who looked at her and smiled. Marlene smiled back. The man leaned forward and spoke: 'Would you like the sugar shaker? I see there isn't one on your table.'

'Oh, thanks anyway,' Marlene replied, 'but I don't take sugar – I like to keep my weight down.'

'Very wise, I must say,' nodded the man, returning to his newspaper.

Sadly, Horace and Marlene never spoke another word to one another: they went on their respective ways never realising they were made for each other, never to know they would have had a lifetime of love and happiness together, would have got married and had two children, a girl named Shirley and a boy named Colin.

SPOILT FOR CHOICE

Ralph Grimstone suddenly found himself between two stools and over a barrel, unable to choose between two women, women so very different in every way that he was spoilt for choice. He thought himself in an enviable position.

Mrs Adelaide Spong had been proprietress of The Old Colonial Tearooms in the village of Quagmire for longer than anyone cared to remember. She kept herself looking smart, as she thought, by the liberal application of mascara and rouge and having her cotton-wool hair regularly bleached at the Sweet Parting Salon in the High Street, her long fingernails were kept up to scratch by regular visits to Cute Claws in the same vicinity. She chose from a wide selection of glittery scarves to hide folds of turkey-gobble skin on her neck.

The Old Colonial Tearooms held the monopoly during holiday seasons when tourists descended on the picturesque town to partake of the famous "Spong's Sponge Pudding". The property itself was decorated in Malayan style, furnished with ancient rattan chairs and wicker tables, and sheaves of pampas grasses gathered dust in large terra cotta pots. The cook was a dowdy grey-faced figure known only as "Cook", and the front of house staff consisted of two elderly females, Miss Pivot and Miss Truckle, who did their best in spite of creeping arthritis and Mrs Spong's peremptory sharp tongue. They wore black dresses, white aprons and frilly caps which were sometimes left unwashed and grubby, a condition not readily noticed by Mrs Spong who refused to wear glasses on grounds of vanity.

The proprietress had been widowed for some years, since which time Ralph Grimstone had automatically stepped in as her occasional escort, or walker, as she preferred to call it. Ralph, ex-Civil Service, harboured a secret longing to marry Mrs Spong and thus acquire a half-share in The Old Colonial Tearooms. He would often lean too close, baring his ultra-white dentures in what he fondly believed was a winning beam. However, this attempt at intimacy irritated Mrs Spong who, in spite of being an instinctive flirt, had never really liked men since the day of her marriage to the late Mr Spong, and she had successfully held Ralph Grimstone at arm's length as, in fact, she had her husband.

Over recent weeks, however, a fly had appeared in the ointment of Mrs Spong's fairly ordered life when Grimstone reported to her one day that a superior catering establishment to be known as The Pink Teapot Café was opening up in nearby Market Square. Evidently a Mrs Heather Cubitt, a newcomer to the area, had bought the premises, previously a high class butcher's shop. Adelaide Spong took this information with a cold feeling in her heart; however, she turned to Ralph with a gracious smile and said "it's a free country, take your tittle-tattle elsewhere", but was obliged to recoil from his nearness and well-meaning grin. She vented her frustration on Miss Pivot and Miss Truckle: 'don't just stand about, wipe those tables down'.

'We just did,' they smirked.

'Well, wipe them again,' she shrieked in reply, flouncing off to apply more lipstick. Pivot and Truckle merely shook their heads knowingly at each other; 'silly old tart' they said behind her back, laughing.

The newcomer, a young-looking female in her early forties, was a different kettle of fish to Adelaide Spong. Heather Cubitt was warm, friendly and outgoing. Ralph took to her immediately and spread the word about the admirable Pink Teapot Cafe, particularly "Cubitt's Cupcakes" as he termed the two pretty young waitresses, Zinnia and Tansy, dressed in pink gingham aprons and matching bandanas tied so loosely that their fine blonde hair showed beneath. There were pink-iced dainties and pink chocolate gateaux set out on multi-layered cakestands, pink gingham tablecloths and serviettes, and pink striped crockery. The pink menu told of luscious buttery snacks and succulent fruit pies with lashings of double cream as well as thick sandwiches with a variety of fillings.

'The Pink Teapot Café, it's a breath of fresh air blowing through this fusty old village of Quagmire,' crowed Ralph to Adelaide Spong, leaning towards her over the counter. Tact was not his strong point.

'Oh, really? Well, we'll see about that,' snapped Mrs Spong. 'People will always go for quality and not some gimmicky fly-by-night flibberty-gibbet.'

'Mrs Cubitt doesn't seem the flighty type, but she is very pretty,' crooned Ralph, not quitting while he was ahead. 'Why don't you let me introduce you?'

'Look here,' grated Mrs Spong, trying not to deepen the frown line between her eyebrows which she had regularly plucked at the Lovely Lashes Salon, 'I'm too busy to stand around listening to your drivel. And, by the way, I won't be going for a drink with you this week, so don't bother calling.'

'Oh, why not?' quizzed Ralph, hiding his teeth in a grimace. 'Was it something I said?'

But Ralph was nothing if not optimistic and he soon perked up when hearing on the grapevine that Heather Cubitt was also a widow-woman and, immediately seeing the possibilities presented, he lost no time in baring his teeth at her and asking her out for a drink at the Akimbo Arms the next evening. Heather Cubitt who couldn't believe she had already acquired a follower, one who, furthermore, might possibly be useful for doing odd jobs for no payment, looked Ralph full in the dazzling dentures and decided to play hard to get as she knew a first refusal would only serve to encourage a keen suitor.

Not that Heather Cubitt was desirous of any soppy stuff and she would therefore have to play it cool if she wanted any work doing around the place as, in her experience, men never seemed content with a platonic relationship.

With a tinkling laugh like a stream flowing over pebbles, she said thank you, she'd take a raincheck and get back to him. But knowing how to keep a man on the boil, Mrs Cubitt added, 'I hope you don't mind if I say what a lovely smile you have.' Ralph was ecstatic. *At last, I have a woman who appreciates me.*

But then he had a brilliant idea. *Why don't I hold a drinks party to welcome the newcomer to the town, invite all the local business people and thereby get my feet under Mrs Cubitt's table?* Ralph realised he was playing both ends against the middle as he was sharp enough to sense that his current amour, Mrs Adelaide Spong, was being a little aloof and this soiree might earn him some brownie points in that department as she could never resist an opportunity of dressing up in her finery.

A large reception room at the Quagmire Inn was duly hired and Ralph Grimstone issued invitations to everyone of importance in the village and in the nearby town of Quorum Thisbé. Adelaide Spong graciously accepted, mainly out of curiosity and not with any goodwill towards the Jenny-Come-Lately who'd had the brass neck to set up her business in direct opposition to the village's long-established tearooms.

The day of the party dawned and Mrs Spong chose her most glamorous beaded dress in tangerine with matching scarf and strappy stiletto heels. She had her nails painted acid green at Cute Claws and her hair was set in a rigid platinum-blonde helmet at Sweet Parting Salon.

Heather Cubitt, in comparison, wore a simple gingham pinafore dress trimmed with linen daisies, set off with wooden beads and flat leather sandals. No two women could have looked more different and Ralph's head was in a whirl, his teeth bared in his most dazzling beam: which lady should he choose to dance with first? As the roomful of party-goers helped themselves to drinks and began circulating, Ralph tapped the table for attention and quickly introduced the newcomer in their midst before requesting the piano and violin duo to commence their musical programme of Viennese waltzes. 'Everyone, please welcome Mrs Heather Cubitt, I hope you enjoy the party and please do tread a measure if you're all sober enough, ahahaha. Miss Truckle, Miss Pivot, please play on!'

To the thin sound of The Blue Danube, Ralph scanned the assembly, wondering which of his ladies to approach and who was most likely to change her name to Grimstone. He was gratified to see Mrs Spong and Mrs Cubitt, his two objects of desire, in animated conversation. *Well, I'm glad they're getting on so well,* he thought, widening his smile as he approached them. *They're probably discussing the various attributes of different puddings and cakes, salads and dips, and when they become great friends, the one won't mind being maid of honour to the other, whichever way it falls.*

In this positive frame of mind, he pushed his way between them. 'Ladies,' he said, 'can I get either of you a drink?'

'Thank you, no,' they chorused, and resumed their conversation, all about M&S, or maybe S&M, Ralph couldn't be sure.

'Well, how about one of you ladies taking the floor with me for a spin,' he crowed. 'Please form an orderly queue and no fighting!' He laughed uproariously, thereby showing off all the dentition in his gaping mouth.

'Oh Ralph, you are a dear,' smiled Mrs Spong. He held out his arms to her.

'No, darling man,' Adelaide continued, 'you've got it all wrong, as usual.' She was shaking her head carefully so as not to disturb her platinum blonde helmet.

Somewhat nonplussed, Ralph realised at least he didn't have to make that difficult decision any more, and he looked towards Mrs Heather Cubitt, the woman he actually preferred now he came to think of it. 'Well,' he said, 'the evening is young – shall we dance?'

'Oh Mr Grimstone – Ralph – we're ever so grateful to you,' said Heather gently, 'but this is how it is, this is the way we are.' And his two objects of desire, gazing deep into each other's eyes, waltzed away in a mist of love, out of his grasp and into a rosy future together.

SUCH A SCREAM

Picture this: Ann and Joy, two smartly-dressed forty-something ladies, sit at a table in an upmarket restaurant; and as we draw near, we overhear them chatting animatedly:

ANN: I must say, this place does an admirable carrot and walnut salad, don't you agree, darling?

JOY: Yes, Ann darling, absolutely marvellous and so low-calorie – plus their spa water with a slice of lime hits the right spot, but, hmm – I see you're picking out your walnuts – if they're going to be left on the side of your plate like that I'll take them home for Yvonne – she adores walnuts, the little darling.

ANN: I still think Yvonne is an unusual name for a bull mastiff, Joy.

JOY: Ye-es, maybe, but she's an individual, like her owner! Oh, by the way, I've been meaning to ask - did you keep the engagement ring after giving Ralph his marching orders?

ANN: No, darling, no, I did not – you'll just die, it was such a scream – I threw the ring in his face with a very dramatic gesture, which I had, of course, rehearsed that very morning!

JOY: How funny! It must have been such a scream, I wish I'd seen it. What did he do?

ANN: Well, you'd have died, you really would – the ring actually hit him on the nose so hard it drew blood (quite a lot of it, in fact, where the stone broke his skin, very freckly skin actually, which I never thought attractive), but anyway, he caught the ring as it fell and he handed it back to me in tears, whether of mental or physical causes, or both, I cannot be certain.

JOY: How clever, darling, the way you handle men. I am full of admiration for your technique.

ANN: Yes – and you'll die when you hear what happened next, it was such a scream – the stupid twit was begging for a second chance as he mopped his wound with that silly monogrammed handkerchief.

JOY: Well, in the twit department, Ralph Grimstone certainly takes the biscuit, but, poor chap, you can't help laughing!! And I hope you kept the ring after all – to add to your collection? How many is it now? It must be five or six, I should imagine.

ANN: I shall have to check my records and come back to you on that, darling. But, oh, as you know full well, I hated the ground Ralph Grimstone walked on. After three months of his bo-o-oring company, I wanted to kill him. I felt it would be immoral to keep anything of his.

JOY: That is very noble of you, Ann darling.

ANN: Yes, is it. I felt very noble, extremely noble.

JOY: So – what happened next?

ANN: Well, Joy darling, you'll no doubt recall that under normal circumstances I prefer to stay on good terms with all my ex-fiancés, but Ralph Grimstone was a different kettle of fish, so pompous and arrogant, no fun at all. I hated the way he jangled the coins in his pocket all the time.

JOY: Absolutely unforgivable, that sort of thing, Ann! A man should be flogged for it! And what did you do next? About him being in tears and begging to be taken back, I mean.

ANN: Oh, I simply spat on the ring and threw it in the river (we were standing on the Millennium Bridge at the time having just viewed the Picasso at Tate Modern – don't go, by the way, it's a load of twaddle).

JOY: Thanks for the tip – I'll wait for the Damien Hirst – the man's a genius: his pickled sheep are simply adorable. But really, you threw the ring in the Thames? I can hardly believe it. What did Ralph do then?

ANN: Well, naturally he looked as if he'd been pole-axed, and let out an animal howl of anguish! Then he stood there peering into the murky depths, moaning at the swirling waters. You'd have died, it was such a scream!!!

JOY: Good grief, you certainly have a strong will to go that far, Ann. But what a waste of expensive jewellery! In your place I'm afraid I should have kept the ring and sold it on if you really couldn't bear to add it to your collection – after all, it must have cost him thousands.

ANN: Oh, I can't lie to you, Joy darling, that's exactly what I did! I sold the original ring weeks ago, and the very kind jeweller made me a duplicate copy in paste and rolled gold. Surely you didn't believe I'd throw a genuine diamond solitaire into the river? *What a scream*!

JOY: Oh, Ann darling, you're a marvel, a girl after my own heart! And what about Ralph? Did you let him in on the joke – put him out of his misery?

ANN: Goodness, no, certainly not. Let the man go on suffering for the rest of his life – that's my philosophy!

JOY: Well said, Ann! Hurrah to that! Now, what might we order for pudding? Shall we celebrate with a water ice?

ANN: Oh, how lovely, darling– I'd just adore a water ice – so refreshing – as long as it's sugar-free.

JOY: Of course, Ann darling, it's sugar-free – you and I, we're sweet enough!

The End

Lightning Source UK Ltd.
Milton Keynes UK
UKOW051157040112

184727UK00001B/5/P

9 781908 481573